DARK PACT

THE MOSTLY OPEN PARANORMAL INVESTIGATIVE AGENCY BOOK ONE

LISA MANIFOLD

Dark Pact

The Mostly Open Paranormal Investigative Agency Book 1

Cover by Atlantis Book Designs

www.atlantisbookdesign.com

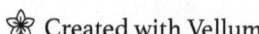 Created with Vellum

Thank you to my lifelong love of Louis L'Amour, who brought me to the old west in the best way possible, and to my new love of the music of Big River Cree, who gave me the inspiration to finish this. I've come home.

The Nightingale/Holliday Family Tree

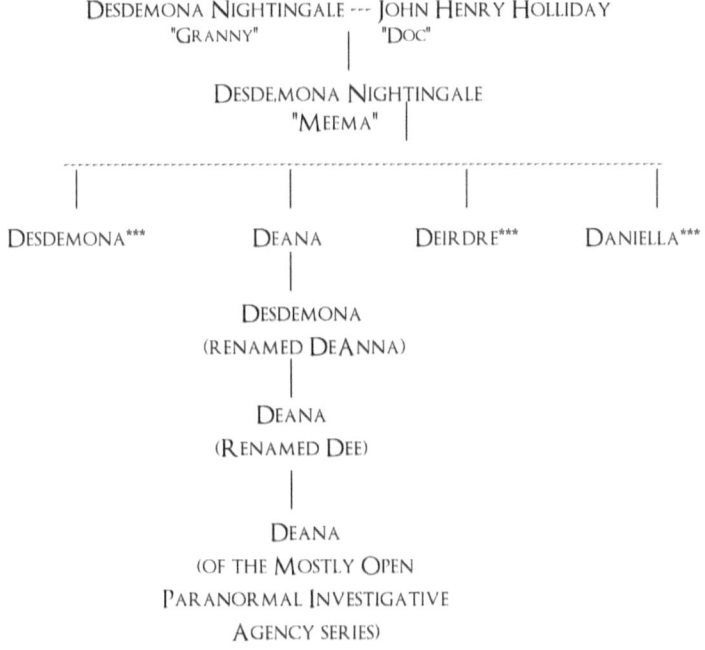

Desdemona Nightingale --- John Henry Holliday
"Granny"   "Doc."

Desde.mona Nightingale
"Meema"

Desdemona***   Deana   Deirdre***   Daniella***

Desdemona
(renamed DeAnna)

Deana
(Renamed Dee)

Deana
(of the Mostly Open
Paranormal Investigative
Agency series)

*** Of the Deadwood Sisters Series

The First Deana
1924
Deadwood, South Dakota

DEANA NIGHTINGALE LOOKED AT HER SLEEPING SISTERS. They'd always been the four Ds. Desdemona, Deana, Deirdre, and Daniella. Her mother—known to one and all as Meema—was a Desdemona as well. Granny had been a Desdemona, too.

It was a tradition, that name.

"To hell with that," she murmured to the night. She would never name her daughter Desdemona. Not after what Granny had told her about that particular name. About all the baggage that came with it.

Well, the ghost of Granny had told her.

If Granny had still be alive, Deana would have kicked Granny down the stairs if she could have—and

Granny had been able to see it, vanishing like her one-time partner, the full-time house ghost, John Henry "Doc" Holliday, did when he was in a snit. Doc had shown up right after Granny vanished. First, he'd been looking for Granny, somehow sensing that her ghost had been around, and then he'd turned his focus onto Deana. He'd questioned her, but she hadn't told him a thing. Deana resolved she wouldn't tell anyone. Not ever, if she could help it.

They all deserved better. But Granny had made sure this whole name business would be a struggle. A life-or-death struggle.

Deana frowned, feeling wrinkles in her forehead. It made her look like an angry guard dog, Deirdre always told her, but given what she knew, it was an appropriate expression.

"I'm going to fix this," Deana said aloud in the quiet room. "Not just for you, Desi. For all of us." She'd been wrestling with telling her sisters, and decided against it. Her heart filled as she looked at her sisters again. How would she go on, being a lone Nightingale?

If she stood here much longer, she'd lose her nerve. She slid the window open, hoping the bike grease she'd rubbed on the window earlier would allow it to open easily—no such luck. The window screeched as she pushed it up.

Her sisters came out of bed like they'd been shot.

"What's going on?"

"Deana, what are you doing?"

"Are you leaving?" That was from Desdemona.

Slowly, Deana turned and braced herself for the performance of her life. "I am," she said, feeling their eyes on her.

"Why?" asked Daniella, her arms crossed.

"I don't want to live a life that someone else chose for me," Deana said, hoping her voice stayed firm. She was afraid she was going to burst into tears, tell them the truth. But her excuse made sense, as Meema had just told them about their responsibilities, and their ability to never die. None of them knew the *truth*, however. The truth was her burden now.

"I'm tired of all the stuff and nonsense that comes from being one of those Nightingale girls," Deana said, rolling her eyes. "I want to go where no one has ever heard of us. And I'm tired of freezing my parts off every winter. I'm going to California, where it's warm. I'm going to live on the beach."

She'd just made that up on the spot, but after she said it, she knew that's what she would do. California was where she was supposed to go.

Silence followed her words. Then Desdemona, always the leader, came forward, and wrapped Deana in her arms. "It's not going to be the same without you, Deana. We love you. Always and forever. Let us know when you get there, and for goodness sake, if you need money, don't be a stubborn mule and refuse to ask." She pulled away, and Deana could see the shiny trail of tears that fell down Desi's cheeks.

Deana started to cry. "I don't want to leave you, but I have to."

"You'll die," Deirdre said.

"We're supposed to die. Us not dying is not normal," Deana shot back. "I accept that."

Daniella came forward, wrapping her arms around Deana and Desdemona, and Deirdre followed.

Deana would never forget it—the moon shining in silver and bright, lighting up the entire room. Her sisters, surrounding her with love. She wrenched away from them, and slid out the window, and down the drainpipe that ran next to their room.

"Love you," she heard from the window. As she looked up, she could see the dark heads of her sisters, their hair falling over their shoulders as they watched her.

"Love you," she said. Deana blew them a kiss, and hurried away, wiping her eyes. "Damn you, Granny," she muttered.

1926
Venice, California

DEANA STRAINED, trying to contain her scream. Whoever said this was going to be overshadowed by the wonder of the baby must have been a man who had no idea what the hell he was talking about because this hurt more than anything she'd ever experienced. It was as though a giant hand grabbed her round the belly and kept squeezing.

"You're almost there," the midwife said. "Keep pushing, that's a good girl." She patted Deana's forehead with a damp cloth.

Deana avoided her gaze, as well as the pitying expression on the assistant midwife's face. They felt sorry for her, a woman having a baby, with no man anywhere to be found.

She didn't need a man. She had herself, and all the skills Meema had taught her. She'd bought a house and was making herbs and tinctures for those in need of help in Venice and doing a booming business in spells to boot. Meema would have taken a switch to her, selling spells, but she needed the work, and it paid better than any secretary's job. It was a secretary's job that had gotten her in the mess in the first place—the boss man brought in a friend who wanted to play footsie, and she'd been too stupid to know the deal. Well, and that friend had known who she was, known her family—but she wouldn't think about that right now. Because right now, she was having a baby.

No, she didn't need the father. She didn't need a man at all. Certainly not *that* one. She was pretty sure he wouldn't be bothering her again. Not unless he wanted a greeting that included her foot in his nether region. Even his kind responded to such things, and she'd make sure it hurt.

"One more," the midwife said, her face red and shining, a grin breaking her stern expression. "The baby's almost here!"

Deana bore down, and she felt the rush of the child come into the world. Tears filled her eyes. She wished she was surrounded by her mother and sisters, but that life was gone.

"What is it?" she asked, letting her head fall back against the bolster.

"A fine girl!" The midwife was gently kneading her belly, helping to finish up the birthing process.

The assistant carried the baby over to the dresser, and cleaned her, carefully wiping the tiny person. The baby wailed, strong and loud, and Deana felt a whoosh of gratitude race through her.

"It's a girl, Meema," she whispered. "Another Nightingale." Even though Deana went by Holliday here in California, she was a Nightingale, and so was her daughter. For good or ill.

"What's her name?" The midwife took the baby from her assistant, now swaddled in a neatly wrapped blanket, and handed her to Deana.

Deana gazed down at the small bundle and saw eyes like her mother's gazing back at her. A chin like her sister's. The baby didn't make another sound after the first wail, just gazed at her, seemingly as fascinated as Deana was.

"Her name is Desdemona," Deana said, hardly knowing what she said.

Then she clapped her free hand over her mouth. *Oh, no.*

LATER THAT NIGHT, after the midwives had gone, promising to return the next morning, Deana leaned over in bed to see where Desdemona—the fourth of the cursed name—lay sleeping in a makeshift bassinet.

"I'm not going let it hurt you, sweet girl," she whispered. "I *will* break it. You're not going to suffer."

She brushed her hand against the soft silk of the baby's head, and then closed her eyes and slid down to sleep.

No one would hurt her baby. Not ever. No matter what Granny had done.

CHAPTER ONE

Present Day
Deana
(Great granddaughter of the first Deana)

It begins, as it always does, with the best, most friendly, helpful of intentions.

The road to utter Hell, that is.

Isn't that how most people get there?

My aunts in Deadwood might have a different opinion, but they're the exception. Most people didn't have a grandmother making deals with demons. I did. Even though that grandmother (known as Granny) is long gone, her choices live on to plague her descendants.

That's not the point. The point is, here I am, fresh off a tangle with a really immense ass of a demon, and I'm right back in the hot seat of a supernatural tangle.

Let me back up a little bit. That road, the one to

Hell? For me, it started with a phone call. On what had already been a weird day.

I'd been back from Deadwood for about two weeks. I'd helped my aunts (who were over one hundred and twenty years old and essentially immortal, as long as they stayed in Deadwood. My great grandmother, also named Deana, had left her sisters and mother and gone to Los Angeles, never to return to Deadwood) defeat a gross demon named Ashlar and discovered just as we took a breath that my aunt Desdemona, and my grandmother, who was originally named Desdemona before she legally changed her name, were both cursed.

Did you get all that? There's a lot of D's in that.

Me being me, I'd insisted that I stay, and help them sort yet another mess out. But all five—all three aunts and my mom and gran—had insisted I come home to Venice.

Before we'd gone to Deadwood for the funeral of my great aunt Meema (the first time I'd ever been to Deadwood, or known much about Great Gran's family), I'd been in the process of opening my private investigative business. I'd gotten my license and had saved enough money to rent a place and open. I even had clients waiting.

So that's what I did. Left Mom and Gran in Deadwood with the aunts who could never die. Opened the Holliday Private Investigations as I'd planned. Everything was going well, going... normally. Until this morning.

This morning, I'd gotten up early and made a pie. I didn't know why, but the pull to get up and bake had been so strong, I hadn't been able to stay in bed. And not just any pie—Smokin' Hawt Cherry Chipotle pie. I'd bought cherries just yesterday on a whim. I had no idea why I had to bake, but I did. I hadn't baked pies since before Derek, my fiancé, had died. Before he died, I baked all the time. And they hadn't even been for Derek. They'd been for one of the members of his band.

One of the things my aunts had emphasized was to listen to my gut. They said now that I knew my history, and had used some of my witch skills, the more I used them, the more they'd grow. Intuition—known as gut instinct—was part of that.

Following my gut, I made the pie, and brought it into work. I cut it into eighths, and waited to see what happened. I couldn't say how I knew something would happen, but I just did. It was my second official day of business. Which is when a call—the call I mentioned earlier—the one that started the road to Hell—came in from my past.

I had no idea as I answered the phone what was coming. Honestly, I was still focused on what the hell the pie and baking urge was all about. "Hello, Holliday Private Investigations, this is Deana, how can I help you?"

A silence and then, "Deana? It's Kel."

I nearly dropped the phone. Kel, formally known as Kelsey Grayson Worthington, was the best friend of my late fiancé, Derek Sinnful (Yes. He really did legally change his name). Derek was the lead singer in Copernicus, and Kel was the drummer. Before Derek died, they were on their way. Since then, they'd gone in a different direction.

So had I. I'd built a lot on being the future Mrs. Sinnful, and it was hard to let go of that. But I'd had to. Derek was gone. I'd lost him.

Derek had been out on a new bike, testing it up in Franklin Canyon park, and someone had hit him, and left him for dead. He hadn't been found until later in the evening. I'd been the one to find him. The cops wouldn't go looking for him, not deeming six hours long enough to be concerned. But I knew something was wrong. I'd known for five of the six hours since he'd left.

I'd just ignored it, telling myself I was worrying too much.

It was because of Derek I'd ended up with my PI license. I wanted to find out who had hit him. So far, nearly three years later, I hadn't. There were no cameras, or any way to trace who'd been in the park that day.

"Kel. It's been a long time. What's up?" I kept my tone level. It was hard. I'd seen Kel every day of my life while Derek and I had been together. He was like family. But after Derek died—everyone fell apart, rather than coming together. Kel and me particularly. I had a particularly large beef with him, but I'd wait to see if I needed to bring that out.

"What kind of investigations do you do?" There was something off in his voice.

"All kinds. What are you looking for?"

His voice lowered to nearly a whisper. "Can I come and see you?"

"Sure. Are you okay?"

"No," he said and hung up.

I sat back in my chair, the thread of worry that had begun when I heard his voice sprouting to full-on worry. I wouldn't have long to wait. He'd be here soon, if he still lived where he had when we'd been friends.

Thirty minutes later, the door swung open, the soft chime I'd installed ringing. Kel came in. He looked at me, and then smiled. "Hey, Dee, how are you?"

I got up and came from around the desk to shake his hand. I wasn't up for a hug. "I'm good."

"This is good to see," he said, gesturing around at my office. "Hey, is that cherry pie?"

Well, isn't this interesting. "It is," I agreed. "But let's not waste time. What's up? You sounded horrible. Have some pie and tell me about it."

He sighed, the smile dropping from his face. He walked to my buffet table where I kept the coffee and today, the pie, put a piece on a paper plate, and sat in the chair in front of my desk. I went back to my chair. This felt bad.

"This is going to sound crazy." He took a bite

mechanically. "But thanks for making my favorite pie. I wouldn't have thought you remembered. How did you know I was going to call you today?"

I shrugged. Internally, I thought, Well, shit. Now I know why I was compelled to bake this morning. I wondered if this was going to become a habit—a pie baking frenzy just before someone rolled into my life. I didn't remember that his favorite pie was cherry, but why would I? I'd done my best to forget all about Kel.

"This is delicious, the extra spice or whatever." He took another bite. "But about why I'm here—my situation—this is crazy," he said again.

He had no idea what my crazy meter looked like these days. "I've seen some pretty strange shit. Just spit it out."

"I went out with a witch," he said.

"Really? A witch? That's unusual?" I asked. I couldn't help grinning.

He looked up and glared. "I'm serious."

I wiped the grin off my face. "So am I. Like, a real witch? How do you know?" Since I'm part witch myself, I wondered how one told a boyfriend. I leaned forward, eager to know. Not that there was a boyfriend on the horizon. I was just interested.

"She told me, and well, after she told me, it was pretty obvious. She dealt with some... interesting characters."

"Really?"

He shook his head as he ran a hand through his

hair. "We dated for a while, and then we broke up, and I ran into someone I'd met coming in her place. That was even weirder," Kel said, stopping to look over my head.

"How?"

He looked down, away from me. "It sounds crazy to even think it." He seemed stuck as to his choice for words.

"No judgement, Kel. Just tell me."

"Lavina was—is—a vampire."

I sat back. I hadn't been expecting that but given my summer so far, I wasn't entirely surprised. Spending time in Deadwood, learning about my family history, meeting my too many times great-grandfather (Doc Holliday, *the* Doc Holliday, if you please!), and any number of other things that happened during the visit to Deadwood left me less ready to clutch my pearls about the unusual than I'd been earlier in the year.

"Okay," I said. "Is that the bad thing that brings you here?"

Kel looked sheepish. "No, it's great—really great, honestly. I like her a lot." He stopped, taking another bite of the pie. "This is delicious," he said again with his mouth full.

Good grief. I was going to have to pry this out of him. "So what's the problem, Kel?" I asked.

"She got into an argument with another vampire, and now that vampire is dead."

"I don't know—"

"They think I did it!" Kel burst out, leaning forward.

He set his plate on my desk. "They took Lavina away to talk to her two days ago, and then last night, three of them showed up at my door and told me I had a week to get my affairs in order and then I was coming with them to stand trial."

"What?" This didn't make sense. It was a huge leap to sleeping with a vampire to becoming a murderer. Not to mention, Kel was—used to be--one of the nicest guys I'd ever met. He was certainly the kindest guy in the band, and I'd been engaged to one of the other guys. Derek had been wonderful, but he wasn't kind like Kel was. Well, like Kel had been. Once Derek died—well, people showed different sides of themselves in death.

"Why do they think you did it?" I asked.

"There's a law against killing other vampires. If you're found guilty, you end up put outside in the daytime, or something like that."

Part of me was just astounded by the fact that I was having this conversation. The practical part of me said, "So they figure Lavina got you, through her feminine wiles, to do her dirty work?"

He nodded. "That's the gist of it. I didn't do this, Deana! You know me!" He picked up the plate again, angrily spearing the pie.

"I did," I said quietly.

He had the grace to look up at me, the fork halfway to his mouth, ashamed. He didn't say anything. What could he say? He was a dick to me when Derek died, and he knew it. He knew I knew it. The fact that I was sitting here talking to him was more of a testament to my feelings for Derek than it was for Kel.

"Look, Deana, I'm sorry—"

I held up a hand to cut off any statements of regret or repentance. They were forced by the situation and empty. "Please don't insult either one of us. Tell me what you want me to do for you, and I'll tell you if I can manage it, and what the price will be."

He paled under his complexion, but he took a breath, and spoke. "I want you to find out who did this. It wasn't me. I wasn't doing anything other than dating a vampire who got into a dust up with another one. That's the only thing I did. Lavina is hot, and sexy, and fun, and I really care about her, but I don't want to die for going out with her."

"Why do you think I can do anything with this?" I asked quietly.

"Because you're the only person I know who does this kind of thing that I can tell the truth to. I'm desperate," he said.

"I figured," I shot back. "How did you know I did this? I've only just opened."

"Look, if you can't help me, just say so," Kel got up. "I was hopeful when I saw your name online."

"I can," I said quietly.

"Are you just saying that? Because I didn't have any idea all these kinds of, of people, existed until this year." He took another bite of pie.

I nodded, thinking it was amazing that this guy was

here in my office, and we were having this sort of conversation while he ate. He was telling me he didn't want to die while he snarfed down my baked goods. "I have connections. But it's going to cost you."

His face took on a wary expression. "How much?"

"Just one 1948 Indian Chief motorcycle, formerly the property of Derek Sinnful. If you haven't sold it for parts by now," I said.

Kel sat down holding his plate tightly, his lips also tight.

Why he hadn't expected that when he called me, much less walked in here was beyond me, but it wasn't my problem. Derek had never gotten around to changing his will, and in the will, which was five years old at the time, he'd given Kel everything. But in anticipation of our wedding, he rebuilt the Indian Chief for me, and it had our initials on it. Kel knew this. All he had to do was give me the Indian as Derek had intended.

Instead, he told me that if Derek had wanted to change his will, he would have, and told me he wasn't doing anything outside of what was specified in the will.

He was right. This was Derek's fault. Derek could have changed it. But he got everything—Derek's stuff, his shares in the band, his place—all I wanted was the bike.

And Kel, once the nicest guy I'd ever met, said no, and shut a door in my face. More than once.

"Deana—"

It was my turn to stand. "If you can't manage the terms of what is agreeable to me, I'm sorry, Kel, but I won't be able to take the job. I'll wish you good luck." I took a few steps around the desk.

"I could die."

"My price is reasonable, given the market value," I said, looking out the window. "And since the bike was personalized, that knocks down overall value." These were all facts that Kel knew.

"I sold it for parts."

"Then my fee will be one hundred thousand dollars, upfront," I said.

"What the hell? No way, Deana! You're out of your fucking mind!"

"Maybe." I shrugged. "Sorry I can't help you, Kel. And I am really sorry, because we were good friends at one point, and I don't think you're a horrible person. You're just an asshole to me." I crossed my arms and waited for him to leave. I could cry later. I wouldn't do it in front of Kel Worthington. Not ever again.

He strode to the door and slammed it behind him as he left. I did notice he took the pie with him. Perhaps the baking was a warning sign of what would be walking into my place. Something to think about. Later.

Right now, I went to my desk and put my head down and cried like Derek had just died.

When I went home that night, I was restless, missing my mom and Gran. Tonight, I was wishing they were here. But I couldn't call them, couldn't add on to their burden. They were trying to save their own lives.

Well, I'd been willing to try and save a life, but he just wouldn't let go of the bike. That was on Kel, no matter how guilty I was feeling. I stared at the television, not really watching it when the ring of the doorbell made me jump.

I padded silently to the door. I opened it to find Kel standing under the porch light, hands in pockets. He looked up and saw me, and without saying a word, stretched his right hand out toward me.

I held out my own hand, and he dropped a set of keys into it. "Meet me tomorrow at your office so I can give you all the information," Kel said, his voice flat.

"Title," I said.

He pulled an envelope from his back pocket and held it out to me. I took it.

"I'm sorry, Deana. Sorrier than you know."

"So am I," I said quietly.

We stared at one another, and then he turned and walked away. I waited until I heard his car leave to go out to the garage.

There in the light, was the Indian Chief. *My* Indian Chief. My bike, restored for me by Derek. Gleaming red, as it had been when Derek painted it. I walked over, and let my fingers trail along the leather seat, still stamped with the "DHS" that Derek had commissioned for it. For what would have been my initials after we married.

And on the gas tank, there it was. The bike was red, with black and chrome accents. But right there in pink and white and silver was a heart with two entwined 'D's'. For me and Derek.

Kel hadn't sold it for parts, or painted over it, or done anything other than kept it. And now, it was with me. I cried a little more as I ran my finger over the initials and the heart, remembering watching Derek paint it. It wasn't perfect, but he wanted to do this one thing that made my bike special, as his gift to me. I'd loved it.

I opened the garage and wheeled the bike in next to my FJ Toyota Land Cruiser, affectionately known as Baby. Now I had Baby and the Chief. As I closed the door, I watched as both of my babies disappeared from view.

Then I went in and went to bed, dreaming of fangs gleaming in the dark all night long.

CHAPTER TWO

I RODE THE CHIEF TO WORK THE NEXT DAY, PARKING RIGHT in front of my office door. As soon as I was done meeting with Kel, I was going to get the new title and tag. I wasn't wasting time with this.

I'll say this—Kel had taken care of her. She purred along exactly the way I'd remembered. Derek had laughed when I told him this was what I wanted, but he'd found one, and it was one of the most gorgeous things on two wheels I'd ever ridden. I loved my FJ Land Cruiser, but that was not ever going to be called smooth and gorgeous. The FJ was more of a beast, which I loved.

The Chief was an indulgence, and I found that I was a little teary when I came into the office.

About twenty minutes after I got there, Kel came in. "Didn't waste any time, did you?" he asked dryly.

"I've been waiting to ride her for a couple of years," I

said mildly, refusing to be drawn into an argument. "You've kept her nice."

"She's beautiful," Kel said behind me.

I turned around to see him with a far less combative expression or demeanor than I expected. "She is," I agreed.

"Can I get some coffee?"

"Go ahead," I gestured at my coffee station. Neither of us spoke as he fixed himself a cup. I noted that his motions were jerky, and he looked tired, as though he hadn't slept.

He sat down across from me and took a large sip. "There's still pie, too."

"Help yourself," I said.

He took another slice. Apparently, it really was his favorite. So. Baking urge equals someone coming into your life. Noted.

"Okay," I said, opening a file on my laptop. "Tell me everything I need to know."

"How do you have a connection?" he asked.

It was a reasonable question. Not one that I wanted to answer, but reasonable. "Let's just say, I've recently discovered I have some family in that sort of business," I said.

His brows drew together. "Vampires?"

"Witches."

"Jesus. I wouldn't have ever thought it," he said. "Although your grandmother was always—" he stopped, seeing the look on my face. "Interesting."

"She still is," I said calmly. "I'm not promising anything, Kel. If you've been around witches and vampires, you know that they operate differently than us," I was talking out of my ass a little here. I didn't know about anything other than the witches and demons I'd recently encountered. Oh, and necromancers. They were all a weird bunch, and that was putting it mildly. I figured vampires would fall somewhere on the 'operate differently' scale.

"You can't even imagine—well, maybe you can. It's so different. Everything—the way they think, act—it's totally different. And it's exciting. Lavina is the most exciting woman I've ever dated. I met her through Phoebe, the witch I was dating." He must have forgotten he'd told me this yesterday.

"How did you manage to meet a witch?" I asked curiously.

"She came to a show, and we had a couple of drinks, and then went to dinner," he shrugged his shoulders. "All of a sudden, we were dating. It didn't last long, but she was a lot of fun. She broke it off," Kel added. "And then after I ran into Lavina, I got a call from from her, asking if I wanted to meet her one night."

"So you've been with her ever since?" I asked.

He nodded as he swallowed the last bite of pie. "You don't cheat on vampires. Not that I would, but they take being together seriously."

"Like she was going to bite you and make you a vampire seriously?" I asked.

"No, not unless... well, no. I've heard of it, but we haven't had that conversation. Which is fine. Anyway, Lavina comes home late one night, and she's furious. I can tell. When I ask her what's up, she said that Jessamine Cassidy was too damn full of herself, and she needed to think about other people." He held up his hands. "That's all I know. That's the extent of it."

"What do you mean?" I asked. "That can't be all."

"It is. Four nights later, these two vampires came to my place, and told her she needed to come with them. She told me not to mention this to anyone, and then she left with them. She didn't even put up a fight, and I've seen her fight. They scared her." Kel took a breath. "Two nights later, they came for me, and there was a third vampire with them, a woman. Elizabeth. That was her name."

"Don't any of these people have last names?"

"Yeah, but they don't matter. They all know each other."

"So what happened when the three vampires came to see you?"

He shuddered. "They—Elizabeth, mainly—told me that I was being taken for the final death of Jessamine Cassidy, and I could come now, and plead my case, or fight, and they'd kill me right then, with no hearing."

"How is it you're free now?" This didn't make any sense.

"I met with some guy, Alfredo—no, Alfonso Delgado, and I explained that I had no idea. He smiled and listened, and said, well, that's all very nice, Mr. Worthington, but humans lie, and so unless you can prove that you had nothing to do with the disappearance of Jessamine, we're going to serve justice. You have one week to collect your proof. And then they hustled me out of there, and took me back to my place."

"When was that?"

"They brought me home right before I called you yesterday."

"So you have six days," I said.

He nodded.

I stood up. "You need to go now. Go and call any and all of your friends who might have seen you on the night in question. What night, exactly, do they think you did this?"

"May twenty-seventh," Kel said.

"All right. Go," I made a shooing motion with my hand. "I can't work with you hovering. I'll call you tonight, and let you know what I've found. You need to make notes about who you talk to, got it? Remember, no promises. Take the pie with you, too."

"I know. But know if you don't help me, I die." Kel's voice was flat.

"I know," I said. I stood, waiting.

He stared at me for a moment, picked up the pie pan, and then swung himself to the door. This time he didn't slam his way out like he had yesterday. That was improvement, I guess.

I sat back down after he'd left. I'd need to call my aunts.

"Hello?" My mom answered the phone.

"Mom, hey—"

"Deana! Honey, it's so good to hear your voice!"

"How's it going with everything?" I asked.

Mom sighed. "Well, it's slow, but we've made progress. We—"

"Mom, let me talk to one of the aunts."

"What's wrong?"

"Well, the weird just walked in my door, and I think they can help me."

"Not there too? I thought we could contain it to just here," Mom said. "Hang on, damn it. Daniella? Can you come and talk to Deana?"

A shuffling on Mom's end, and then I heard Daniella's voice. She was the calmest of all three of my aunts. Deirdre had the temper, and Desdemona was the bad ass. I wouldn't want to face off against any of them. They were fierce.

"What's up?" Daniella asked.

"Who do you know that's a vampire that will talk to me?" I asked. I explained my case from a high level, and then Daniella sighed.

"Vampires are kind of a pain in the ass. They're usually really proud, like big balls of ego and they talk too much. The older ones are a lot more formal, so if you talk to any of them, you need to remember that. Manners go a long way. Even you, with your witch ancestry, are still part human, so they will look on you as fairly unenlightened," she finished.

"One of the ravaging hordes?" I asked dryly.

"Something like that," Daniella said. "Let me check with Des—I think I know who to send you to." She covered the receiver and I could hear her yelling.

301 Pearl Street, the family home in Deadwood, was not usually a quiet place. I waited, hoping like hell this would have a chance at working. I might have been pissed as hell at Kel, but I didn't want him to die. Not if he didn't do anything that he should pay with his life for, and while he had been a complete asshole to me, I didn't get murderer off him.

My gut was usually right on, only giving me problems when I ignored it. When Kel had come in yesterday, I'd been thinking about how to manage forgiving him, and struggling. It had only been a bike. And then my anger had come roaring back.

"Okay, you have something to write this down with?" Daniella asked.

"Yeah, hang on," I took down the information she gave me.

"Email him. Do it right now. He's got people that protect them during the day, so someone will read the message and give it to him tonight. Tell him we recommended that he speak with you, if he's so inclined, and you'd really appreciate fifteen minutes of his time."

"What the hell am I going to ask him?" I asked. This was moving fast, and I felt like I was falling behind.

"Ask him what the evidence is, who accuses your friend, and why they think Lavina would have done this. Those are the three things. Then maybe you can talk to the witnesses."

"Oh, great. More vampires."

"Carry your spell bags," she said. We'd made all kinds of spell enhancing bags when I was in Deadwood —I called them the magic tea bags—and I'd been carrying them with me ever since. You shouted out a spell while you toss the bag and boom! Magic happens. At least, it's supposed to. I'd never used them, outside of practicing with my aunts.

"You can use the slow down, and the fire bags," Daniella continued. "Most vampires aren't magic, although some, like Jessamine, and maybe your friend's girlfriend, dabble in it. Actually, Jessamine was a skilled scryer."

"You mean like seeing stuff in water?"

"Exactly that, and she was usually right. If she read for you, you paid attention."

"Did you ever meet her?"

"No," Daniella said. "She had a husband, mate is what they call it in vampire world, and they are older than we are. They never came through here."

If Jessamine and her man hadn't come through Deadwood, my aunts would not have met them. They were witches, and they were immortal, but they only retained their power and their immortality if they stayed within Deadwood. That would make me crazy, but then, I'd never left the house I grew up in here in Venice, and I never wanted to leave the Los Angeles area. I had enjoyed Deadwood more than I thought I would, and not just for family connections. There was a peace I hadn't expected to find there.

"Thanks, Daniella. Tell me the truth. How are things going?"

"Challenging, but nothing the Nightingales have to do is ever easy," she sighed. "And we can't keep enough bacon in stock for Beeval."

Beeval was their resident house demon. Who was the best of friends with Evil, their resident house chicken. I laughed.

Daniella continued, "These are, however, first world witch problems, and we're fine. Don't worry about us, Deana. Just take care of yourself, and never, ever trust the vampires to back you up against one of their own. Got it?" Her voice was low and serious.

"Got it."

"And know that they don't do anything for free. If Zachary gives you his time, he will expect some of yours."

"Shit. Like, in what way?"

"He'll want a favor. Vampires are very into favors. If he asks, which he will, only agree to something that can be done within the week. Do not---I repeat, do not— allow him to talk you into owing him something at a later date."

"You're scaring me."

"Good," Daniella said. "Fear's a good guide."

"Thanks, I think," I said.

"Hey, you're a bad ass. You have nothing to worry about. I'm giving you a heads up on the rules so they don't try to pull on over on you."

I felt better with her reassurance. "Thanks, Daniella."

"Let me know if Zachary doesn't get back to you. I'll give him a nudge. Love you," she said.

"Love you, too. Tell everyone."

"I will." Daniella hung up.

I felt better after making that small connection with my family. The house was lonely without Mom and Gran, even as I knew they needed to be there, working on breaking the family curse. I opened my email and sent an email to the vampire she'd given me info for, and then settled in to wait. I'd added my phone number, in case he wanted to call, but it was hours before dark, so I had some time to kill.

After an uneventful lunch, the chime on the door rang. I looked up, and an older man, tall, lanky and with a face that was wrinkled from the sun came in. He was neatly dressed in jeans and a flannel shirt, and he carried a beat up looking brown paper bag under his arm. He looked to be of Native American ancestry, with dark eyes that were lively, and as he turned a little to close the door behind him, I could see he had a long, neat braid down his back.

"Can I help you?" I wasn't sure what to make of him.

There was something about him that made my witchy sense tingle. I slid a hand into the pocket of my jeans where I had the fire tea bags. Fire would hold off most of the things that went bump in the night, even if they walked around during the day.

"I'm looking for Deana Holliday," he said, his voice deep, with an accent I couldn't place. It was as though English wasn't his first language.

"I'm Deana," I said, standing, and extending my right hand, keeping the tea bag clutched in my left down by my leg.

He appraised me slowly, looking me over from head to toe. Even though he couldn't see my toes, I felt the intensity of his scrutiny. "So you are," he said. "I think I'd like to hire you."

"You're not sure?"

"Well, I'd like to speak with you to be sure," he said.

"Please have a seat, then," I said, gesturing toward my desk.

He sat down carefully, still holding the bag. He saw me looking at it and slid it under the chair near his feet.

"Can I get you something to drink?"

"Water, please," the man said.

Neither of us spoke while I got him a bottle. Handing it to him, I sat down across from him. Part of me was anxious to get to work on checking to see if there was an email from Zachary, seeing if he had any online presence, but you can't turn down business when it walks in the door. The other part of me felt like this was about to be something big. I slid the fire bag I'd been holding into my pocket, but at the top in case I needed to get to it in a hurry.

The man looked around. "This is neat, and tidy. Like yourself."

Okay. "Thank you," I said.

"But you need some food."

"I'm sorry, I only have beverages," I said. Too bad I'd let the pie walk out the door earlier. Something told me this guy would have appreciated it.

He nodded as he opened his water bottle. "It'll do. Now you are able to find someone?"

"It depends on who you're looking for, but that is my job," I said.

He nodded. "Makes sense. I'm looking for someone that I think might be my daughter."

"What are your plans if she is?"

"Is that your business?" His dark eyes bored into me.

"Well, no, but it's part of my ethics. I'm not going to stalk someone for you," I said before I realized it. And while I hadn't thought about it, this was part of my ethics. Good to know. Might have been nice to know this before I opened a business. But my gut told me I needed to say this.

He looked at me for a moment, and then nodded. "I can appreciate that, Deana Holliday."

"Why are you trying to find her?"

"I was in a relationship with her mother years ago,

and I've only been made aware of the existence of the child—well, woman now—recently," the man said.

"What's your name?" I asked.

"Caleb Baker."

"Mr. Baker, why don't you give me the details about this woman, and her mother, as you know them?"

He leaned back, and I opened a file on my laptop for him. It seemed straightforward, and honestly, I didn't get creeptastic vibes from him. I did, however, feel I needed to warn him of my boundaries. He was pleasant, and easy to talk with, so I didn't think he minded.

At the end of an hour, he stood up, pulling the paper bag from under his chair. "I think I shall hire you, Deana Holliday. You have my contact information, so please let me know what you find at the end of the week."

He'd just now decided to hire me? What had we been doing for the last hour when I could have been composing the perfect response or explanation email to a vampire? Not that I'd heard from him yet, but I would. And I was worrying over what to say, how to proceed. "Um, okay. We haven't discussed my fee."

Caleb pulled a wallet from his back pocket and took out a stack of bills. "There is five thousand there." He set it on my desk. "That should cover your expenses."

"Well, yes, but—"

"I shall expect to hear from you by week's end," Caleb said, and walked out of the office.

I leaned back, pulling the money toward me. When

I'd talked with other PIs, this was not the norm. In fact, not being paid was the norm, and so far, I hadn't had to chase anyone for payment.

There was something *other* about Caleb Baker. Maybe he was part of the new community that I found myself part of? I shook my head. Since coming home from Deadwood, I was seeing the boogeyman everywhere I looked, and while I did think that the supernatural world was larger than I'd realized, I didn't think it was a bad guy around every corner.

I took the time to finish my notes, and then closed Caleb's file for the time being. I needed to get to the Motor Vehicles department before it closed. My need to worry about all my latest clients would have to wait.

CHAPTER THREE

AFTER I'D FINISHED MAKING THE CHIEF LEGALLY MINE AT Motor Vehicles, which had gone more smoothly than any other time I'd been there ever, I spent the rest of the afternoon running down information based on what Caleb had given me. The email to Zachary was sent, and all there was to do was wait. At seven, I locked up, and headed back to our house on the canal. I kept checking my email, but even after the sun set, there was nothing.

Well, nothing that I wanted to see.

I'd added my phone number, so maybe he'd just call. At ten after ten, my cell rang. "Hello?"

"Deana Holliday?" A male voice I didn't recognize asked.

"Speaking."

"This is Zachary Ennis. I received your email inquiry today."

"Thank you for getting back to me so quickly," I said. "I appreciate it."

"You have, on the strength of my connection to your aunts, asked a favor of my time. I'm a busy man."

"I realize that," I said.

Before I could say more, Zachary continued. "I have great affection for the Nightingales, so I shall be able to meet you for half an hour this evening."

"Great. Where?"

He named a bar just north of me. "You're in Venice?"

"No, but you are," he said. "In an hour, please." The line went dead.

Whoa. He knew where I lived. I didn't know how I felt about that. I'd decide when I met him.

Since I'd gotten ready for bed, I had to get myself together again. I chose my favorite leather jacket, even though such a thing is almost silly in California, but I was riding the Chief—now sporting a new license plate and title—and the jacket was a necessity.

The Venice Ale House was dimly lit, and not all that busy as I pulled into the parking lot. I wondered how I'd know Zachary.

That wondering lasted all of thirty seconds once I walked in the door. At a table toward the back sat a blond man, tale, pale, and flanked by two muscle guys, also tall and pale.

"Don't even need a name tag," I muttered.

The man at the table stood up and nodded at me

from across the room. As I walked over, I could feel the eyes of all three men on me.

"No, you don't need a name tag. You look a great deal like your Nightingale relations," the man said. "I am Zachary Ennis. Please join me."

As I slid into the booth, he said, "Would you care for something to drink?"

"A water, please."

He nodded at one of the muscle guys, who moved to the bar. It was like watching ballet in action. I'd never met any vampires, and Kel's fascination with his girl-friend made sense.

"I appreciate the discretion you showed in your email, Miss Holliday," Zachary said.

Jerking my attention from the guy at the bar, I looked at Zachary. "Please call me Deana. Miss Holliday feels like my grandmother is here."

He smiled, and the smile changed his face entirely. He was handsome, in a very angular way. Sharp cheek-bones, sharp straight nose—and the smile eased the planes of his face. "Of course. So now that we are here, because I value your Nightingale relatives, how can I help you?"

"It is, as I mentioned, a matter of some delicacy," I started. I'd been practicing this one for a while in my head, ever since I'd sent the email. "I would like to know what it is that has convinced your leadership that Kel Worthington ended the life of Jessamine Cassidy."

I'd decided in the end that polite honesty was my best approach.

Zachary sat very still. "You are correct. This is a matter for delicacy. I must ask, since you are being so open with me, what is your concern in this affair?"

"Kel Worthington is my friend. He says he had nothing to do with Jessamine other than knowing that his friend Lavina had some sort of disagreement with her."

One eyebrow went up across the table from me. Then Zachary looked over. "Ah, Peter, thank you. Perfect timing," he said.

Peter set a glass of water in front of me and moved away. This was starting to feel like I was walking on a tightrope. I felt my heartbeat speed up, and a little bit of sweat between my shoulder blades.

"Friendship aside, I don't see how it's your business."

Shit. I'd thought about this too. "Well, you have a point. But you all need to get along in this world, and it doesn't really look good to be killing off humans without absolute proof."

"How do you know there is no absolute proof?"

"Honestly?" I asked.

He nodded.

"Well, I've had my issues with Kel. I'm saying that because if you look around, you'll know it. Better to get that out front. But he's not a killer."

"Just a shit who keeps other peoples' things?" Zachary asked.

Holy hell. "Wow. I envy your info network," I said, keeping my tone even.

"I believe in being prepared. It was easy enough to find," Zachary shrugged.

I laughed. "Yeah, I'm sure it was. I was pretty vocal about how angry I was at him. But it should say something that I'm willing to stick my neck out for him. He was a shit to me, but that doesn't mean he murdered anyone."

"That may be, but people will do a lot of things for those they love."

"Do you mean me, or Kel?"

"Both?" Zachary raised both brows this time.

"Is this information that is available to me? Before whatever punishment is carried out?"

"That's right, he is on a deadline, isn't he?" Zachary leaned back.

"That's one way to put it," I said.

He smiled briefly and then sat still. Hopefully he was considering how to help me and not how to kill me fast and hide the body.

"Your point about not making waves in the human community has merit. Who knows how many people he's told about this?" His eyes met mine, and he rolled them. "I have no issues with vampires getting together with humans, but the humans need some discretion."

"Threat of dying kind of loosens the tongue."

Zachary smiled, a real one. "That's true. I've seen enough die to know better." He tapped his finger against his lips.

I sat and tried not to react to how casually he dismissed human death. I hoped I was keeping my face calm and expressionless. And I waited. It would be bad manners to push. I didn't know how old Zachary was, but manners never hurt, and I could hear Daniella's words in my ear.

He leaned back finally. "Normally, I wouldn't involve myself in this, but I do think your concern is worth some allowances on our part. If you cannot prove your friend innocent, he will die." His eyes, dark and cold, met mine.

I nodded. "I understand that."

"Does he? If he runs, we will find him. And Lavina will pay the price as well."

"I'll pass that on to him."

"Please do. Now, as for help. I am, as I said, willing to make some allowances, but I cannot have you, even a human such as yourself, to careen around our community, making a fuss."

"That's not really my style," I said.

He smiled. "No, it doesn't seem to be, but one never knows. I'll send one of my associates to you. Tonight. Do you have somewhere safe for sleeping once the sun rises?"

Oh, wow. I hadn't planned on having a vampire in my house. "Um, yes. I do." We had a room that was originally intended to be a wine cellar. I could drag a bed into there.

"Excellent. I am trusting you with my associate, and I hope you will appreciate such a trust. You will also listen to their advice as to how to proceed, do you understand?"

I nodded.

"Now, in return, I shall require a favor from you, Deana," Zachary said, inclining his head toward me.

"I am happy to do so. I request that you make it something I can do within the week."

He stared, and then he burst out laughing. "You've been well schooled, I see. I do love your aunts. Very well. I actually do have something I need help with, and my own... associates have not been able to make progress on this matter."

"I'll do all I can," I said.

"I am sure you will, Miss Holliday. I believe that the human police may need to be brought in, but I feel certain I can count on your discretion?" His eyebrow went up.

"Of course."

Zachary gave me the particulars of what he wanted me to find for him. Then he told me to expect his associate later tonight, and suggested that I might like to go home now. I took the hint, and hauled ass out of there.

My home was nice—we'd moved from the cottage my great-grandmother had originally bought when I was still a baby. They all felt that I deserved a nicer place, and this one looked like it had come out of a fairy tale, like a chateau in the French countryside. I loved it. I loved living on one of the canals. So I had nothing to be ashamed of there. But I found that I was nervous, and moved around the house once I'd dragged a bed into the former wine cellar. The only other supernatural people I'd been around had been related to me, and liked me. They weren't potentially going to kill me.

A light knock at the door nearly made me jump out of my skin. I hurried to answer it, and when I did, I saw a tall, willowy woman with light hair stood in the doorway.

"Can I help you?" I asked.

"I am looking for Deana. Zachary sent me," she said.

"I'm Deana."

"Can you invite me in? I don't like being out on the street."

I stood back, allowing her room to come in.

"You have to say it," she said.

Oh. "Please come in," I said.

She moved in past me, moving faster than I expected. Again, like watching ballet, except the ballet dancer was in speed motion.

She was slight, but wiry. Her hair was light blond, and I could tell that she'd been fair and pale before she was a vampire. She faced me, her eyes dark, and hard, at odds with her almost fae like appearance. "What is it you need from me? Zachary told me to come and help you, and that once you gave me the task, you'd listen to me as to how it is carried out."

No beating around the bush here, was there? "I need to speak to Alfonso Delgado, among other things."

Her only reaction was to raise an eyebrow. "Why?"

"Because my client thinks Delgado has something to do with the matter he's hired me to solve. In fact, I know he does, but that's one place to start looking for some answers." This would need to happen fast. As of midnight tonight, Kel was down to five days.

She nodded. "I get Zachary's instructions now. How familiar are you with vampires? And what are you?"

"I'm part witch, according to history, and I'm not sure what you're asking. Like, how vampires go about their business?"

"That's exactly what I'm asking. And there's something more than just a witch."

"How can you tell?"

"There's something more. We have an excellent sense of smell."

"Oh." I nodded, crossing my arms. "What's your name?" I wondered what she smelled to ask what else I was—but this didn't seem the time to ask. "And what else do you smell?" I couldn't seem to help myself.

"My name is Tuesday. As to you, I'm not sure. It's..." she stopped, and inhaled deeply. "It's not human. Or witch. You have no idea?"

"No. I wish I did. Thank you for coming to help me."

I wanted to change the subject of me. This made me nervous.

"I didn't have a choice, but if you're going to give Delgado a headache, I'm happy to help."

"What's your beef with him?"

"He killed my partner." Her words were flat and stark.

"I'm sorry."

"I'm not allowed to kill him." Her eyes were even darker.

I didn't think that was possible. "I don't want to kill him." I needed to clarify that.

"That's all right. I enjoy the thought of giving him a business headache," she smiled, and her fangs were visible.

She was scary as hell. If I met her in a dark alley, I'd pee my pants. Without even a second thought. She might be slight, and wiry, and look like a tall fairy, but right now she looked like she could kick the ass of an entire football team, and not even break a sweat.

"Where can I sleep?" Tuesday asked.

"I have a place in the back of the house. There aren't any windows, and," I walked to the back room, "I set up a bed for you. I wasn't sure what you'd prefer."

Clicking on the light, I showed her where I'd set up the bed. "Will this be comfortable for you?" I asked. I hadn't had to put up a vampire before.

"This is acceptable," Tuesday said, her voice softer than before. "Thank you for taking the trouble."

"It's no trouble," I said. "I want you to be able to sleep safely."

"Dawn is still some hours away. Shall we talk about what else you feel you need?"

"That would be great. I'm kind of on the clock, here," I said.

"How so? Zachary did not tell me the particulars, so I would appreciate if you could tell me everything you know."

I walked back to the kitchen. "I'm sorry," I said, turning to face her. "I didn't think about anything to eat for you—"

"I have addressed that," Tuesday said very formally. "But thank you."

Daniella hadn't been kidding. The manners thing was big so far with the two vampires I'd met. "Well, have a seat." I gestured at the large table.

She sat, and I told her the story that Kel had told me. Her eyes narrowed slightly at the mention of the murdered vampire.

"This friend is worth you getting involved?"

I shrugged. "He was, once. He's not a bad guy. Generally."

Tuesday smiled, but there was no warmth in it. "They're all bad guys at times, Deana Holliday. But that is not on me to judge. I know Lavina and knew Jessamine somewhat."

"What did they fight about?"

Tuesday shrugged. "I don't know. I heard about it, of

course. The community here is not that large, and Jessamine is well known. All I know is that both were angry."

"Like killing angry?"

Tuesday looked at me for a moment, and then said, "There is a great deal of fallout that would land on a vampire who kills another."

"So is that a no?"

She shrugged again. "I don't know. Lavina has a pretty horrible temper. Jessamine was far calmer. She's older, and her mate would not allow Lavina to threaten her."

"Would her mate be a threat to Jessamine?" I had to ask, and what better person to ask than someone who knew them, but had no dog in the fight.

"Vampires only mate when they are very sure, but it's a fair question. However, knowing her mate, I will say no."

I sighed. "This doesn't look good for Kel. Is Lavina the type to get someone else to do her dirty work?"

Tuesday pressed her lips together. She didn't want to give me her full opinion of Lavina.

Which made sense. Kel tended to date what I'd call crazy chicks. It looked like he'd upped the stakes since we'd last been friends. "Got it. No need to say more."

"Why don't you go to bed, and I'll see what I can find out?" she asked abruptly.

"Um, well, okay. Thanks for that."

"Of course."

LISA MANIFOLD

"Is there anything else you need tonight?" I asked.

"I am fine," Tuesday said. Thank you."

Leaving her in the kitchen, I went up to my room. I wasn't afraid of Tuesday. But her presence in my house made me afraid of what came with her; what I'd gotten myself into.

Tonight, as I crawled into bed, I pulled the blankets up to my chin, and burrowed into the pillows.

It was that kind of night.

CHAPTER FOUR

I woke the next morning, far earlier than I ought to have, given the lack of eight hours of sleep. *There's a vampire in my house* was my first thought. Then, *I still have to go to the office today.* My clients were stacking up, and that was just on the supernatural side of things.

Normally, I like to take my time in the morning, but today, I hurried. As I unlocked the door to my office, I realized I hadn't been in this early since I'd opened the doors. I made coffee and got right to work. My email had a number of requests, and while most were things I wouldn't be able to help with, there were a few that I responded to for more information.

Then I turned my attention to Caleb Baker and his request. I did a search for him, first. He turned up in only one of my searches—PIs having access to a little more information than your standard Google search. He was a witness to a horrible accident nearly twenty-five years ago the same year the girl he thought might be his daughter had been born. He'd been a witness when a building in Minneapolis collapsed. Most of the people were all right, but one office—a brokerage firm—had lost almost two-thirds of their employees.

The FBI later found that the employees who had died were involved in a major Ponzi scheme, targeting the elderly. The FBI notes were not anything out of the ordinary, although they were impressed with Caleb's calm demeanor and his willingness to help the victims in the aftermath of the collapse.

That should have comforted me, but it didn't. It fed into my thoughts that there was something more about Caleb Baker. I resolved to ask him when we touched base again, although I wasn't sure how that conversation would go.

Shaking my head, I took a look at the women he'd given me information on. The mother, and her daughter. I pulled birth records, and then I sighed. There was no way—well, no legal way—that Caleb was the father. First, another man—the woman's ex-husband—was listed on the birth certificate. Second, the mother was here in Los Angeles, and the conception must have happened while Caleb was pulling survivors from the rubble of the aforementioned collapsed building, if my counting backwards nine months from the baby's birth was correct.

The FBI had kept track of him for two months after the accident. He hadn't left the area, and he would have had to come here, to Los Angeles, in order to be a father, biological or legal. Which, according to the FBI, hadn't happened. He hadn't left Minneapolis at all. Not for the conception, or the birth.

Better to get this over. I dialed the number he left me.

"Deana Holliday," his deep voice answered on the third ring.

"Hello, Mr. Baker," I said.

"You have information?"

"I do. I do not believe you are the woman's father," I said. It was always better to rip the band aid off quickly.

"You have reasons for this belief?" he asked.

"I do."

"Then I shall come and see you, and you can show them to me."

"I'll be happy to send you the infor—" I stopped. He'd hung up. Well, okay then. I got the information in order and set it aside. Open and shut in less than two days. I went to my safe to get his money, sliding it into a manila envelope. My bill wouldn't come to anything near what he'd left me.

The bell on the door rang and I looked up, expecting Caleb Baker. It was Kel, and he looked terrible.

"Deana! What have you found?" he asked.

"I have a meeting set up with Delgado," no sense in telling him I didn't have it yet, but that I would, "And I'm working on why it is they think you did it."

He dropped into the chair in front of my desk, running his hands through his hair.

"What does Lavina say about this?" I asked.

"I haven't seen her since they took her away. She texted me, and told me to tell the truth, but she didn't send me to do anything."

"Was she really angry at Jessamine?"

He shot a sharp look at me. "She was. I'd never seen her so angry. She kept saying, 'II can't believe she's doing this!' and a couple of times she kicked things across the room. But she wasn't just angry."

"Oh?" This would have been nice to know when he came in here.

"Yeah. She was mad, and she was also scared."

"How can you tell?" I tried to keep the skepticism out of my tone. From the vampires I'd met, I didn't think they'd show fear. And especially not to a human, no matter how much he might have rocked her world between the sheets.

"It was her eyes. She's always so calm, even when she's pissed. And she has a temper," he shook his head, the corners of his mouth turning up. "But her eyes were afraid."

"You're sure?"

"No," he said, staring at me. "But I've been with her for nearly a year. And we've... well, we've..." he stopped.

"You need to be honest with me," I said.

"We've shared blood," Kel whispered. "Once we did,

I could tell how she was feeling more. Like, I could look at her, and get a sense, you know?"

"No, I don't. But I'll take your word for it. Is this something that's not allowed?"

"I don't know. She told me not to talk about it. So maybe?" He shrugged. "There's less than five days, Deana. You have to help me!"

"Kel, I'm doing everything I can. It's tough when some of the people I have to speak with only work at night, but I should have some more info tonight. I can't have you up my ass, either. I'm already suspect because I'm human, and I'm standing up for you."

That had come out without me meaning to say it, but it was true. And he should know what he was asking, even if he had paid what I asked. I might not be around to enjoy the Chief next week if I went wrong on this one.

He didn't say anything.

"Now I need you to go home. Get your shit in order. Just in case things go bad. I don't think they're going to, but it's going to be a close thing," I said, realizing that my words were exactly what I thought. I stopped, because the feeling that came over me as I spoke was... indescribable. I didn't know how I knew, but I knew.

Whatever he saw in my face, as well as my words, must have convinced him. He got up. "Thank you, Deana. I know I don't deserve it. I know I was a shithead to you. I hope you can forgive me."

"It's the past, Kel. And you've done what I asked to

make things... better," I finished. I'd been about to say 'right', but I didn't think things would ever be right between us. And that was okay. They didn't have to be. We were both doing the best we could to do the right thing.

That would have to be enough.

Kel left, and I leaned back. I hoped I hadn't been just talking out of my ass when I told him that things would work out. It felt right—it still felt right. I had no idea why. Current affairs didn't seem to back that up. While I was contemplating this, the bell on the door rang again.

Caleb Black walked in, a brown paper bag tucked under his arm, just like when I'd met him. I got up and held out my hand. He took it, and I felt a surge of power that radiated from him.

Yep. There was definitely an other. As he sat down in front of my desk, I walked over, turned the sign to Closed, and locked the door, pulling the blinds on the it.

Caleb turned around. He looked amused. "Is that necessary, Deana Holliday?"

"It is. You know, in addition to Holliday," I'd thought this over carefully, "I have another family name." I came back around and sat down behind my desk, not breaking eye contact.

He raised his eyebrows but didn't respond.

"It's Nightingale. I have three aunts who live in

Deadwood. You might say they are a fixture there." I leaned forward. "Perhaps you've heard of them?"

"I have. They are, in my opinion, a positive addition to Deadwood."

"I think so, too. So with that, it's time for honesty, Mr. Black. What are you?"

He smiled then, and it was genuine. "I wondered how long it would take you to figure it out. You're very good."

I shrugged. "I have good research."

"So you know that I could not be the father of the young lady that I gave you information on?"

"Not unless you snuck out from under FBI surveillance and flapped your wings back here."

Caleb nodded. "No, I did not. I wanted to see how you would react, and you have behaved admirably. I was also not sure if you were able to sense others like us."

"What if I hadn't?"

He shrugged. "I would have paid you, thanked you for your time, and moved on."

"What do you want, Mr. Black?"

He leaned back, looking off at the wall. "I've been alive a long time. Not as long as some of the other mystic folk that walk this Earth, but for me, it's been a long time."

"How long?" I asked.

"I began my walk over two hundred years ago. I was created, brought here, to help my people."

"Who are your people?"

Caleb sighed, and in that sigh, I saw the age on him. He went from a middle-aged man to one who was ancient. I blinked.

"I'm dying," Caleb Black said. "And like anyone, human or otherwise, I have my secrets. Except this one, I cannot take to the grave with me. Finally, I must share my story."

CHAPTER FIVE

I DIDN'T KNOW WHAT IT WAS, OR HOW HE DID IT, BUT THE mood in my small office had shifted. I felt that I was outside, in the great wide-open plains. I could almost feel the wind in my hair.

Then Caleb began to speak. "I was created by a great medicine man, of what you would know as the Heart Lake First Nation, of the Alberta Cree. He was a shaman, a man who understood that a shift was coming to the people. Matunaagd, my father, saw what the white man would bring us. And so, he created me, named me *Kisemanitokatew*, to help *Iyiniwok*, the people, find their way when the darkness came to take their spirits. I served him, and the people, well. I returned the good to their spirits, banishing those things of evil." He stopped, and the pain on his face made the tears spring to my eyes.

"You would call me a wendigo. A wendigo is the

closest thing to describe what I am, without the negative of that creature. There are no words. My name means the great, good positive force in the universe. I was created to bring that to those who had lost it or were in danger of losing it. My people needed that, after the white man came."

I didn't know what to say. I knew that the U.S. had a pretty shameful track record with the people who were here first but hearing it like this—it was though a weight had been laid upon my shoulders.

"When Matunaagd passed onto the spirit world, I rejoiced, because then I would once more see my father, my *Kôhtâwiy* . But I did not. He passed on without my ever having seen him. The mourning of his loss went on for a year, and all his possessions were given away. After that year, I was there for the feast that honored his passing, and still, I did not see him. I didn't know what to do. I was as a child who has lost his parents and is unaware of the world." He looked at me then. There were tears in his eyes. "Matunaagd had told no one of me. Therefore, there was no one to guide me, and I was left to find my own way. The years after his death were the darkest of my existence." His gaze traveled over my head.

"Needless to say, Deana Holliday, I found my way."

"Uh... not to be disrespectful, but don't wendigos eat people?" I thought I was remembering it right.

"They do. I ate the evil spirits that would inhabit men, that would make them harm others. I gave the room for the positive spirits that they needed to heal the human heart."

"Have you eaten lately?" I asked, wondering if I was stepping over a line. I also wondered what the hell this had to do with me, and my case.

His now-ancient eyes bored into me, and then he laughed. It was a laugh that came from the soul, from the depth of being. This was a good thing—at least it increased my chances of not being eaten, I supposed.

"I have, indeed. There are many evil spirits poised above the people of this city. Most, I cannot help. They do not wish to be saved. They invite the evil. But those who do not—I help. I take the evil spirits within and allow room for the good spirits to find their home."

"That's a good—"

He held up a hand. "My story is nearly done, Deana Holliday. Over the years, I have found myself in the company of others like myself—not of this world. It has allowed me to walk my own path, do what I think is best. To do as my *Kôhtâwiy* would wish me to. I serve more than just the *Iyiniwok* now, although they are the people of my heart. I have done what I could for them, and I can see my own death. It is time for me to pass on."

"Are you sure this is the end for you?" I asked.

He nodded. "I am. As I told you, my customs are that when a man goes to the spirit world, his possessions must be disbursed of. I heard of your encounter with your aunts in Deadwood."

"Does the supernatural world have some kind of newspaper or something?"

"We have message boards," Caleb said, sounding like any other man in Los Angeles today. "And we talk. Your aunts are well known, and well-thought of. I am partial to them, although I have never met them. They will protect their land, their tribe—no matter who is in it. And you are a Nightingale." He regarded me somberly. "That is why I think you will do."

"I'll do for what?" I asked.

"What do you know of your heritage?" Caleb asked, taking a conversational turn.

"I'm a Nightingale, and a Holliday, and I've studied with my aunts."

"I will help you to better understand who you are," Caleb said.

A thought occurred to me, harking back to my conversation with Tuesday last night. "Is there more?"

"More?"

"More to me than my witch ancestry."

He studied me. "There is, although I cannot see what it is."

I sighed. "You're the second person whose mentioned it to me recently."

"I will try to help you discover it, and I will also help you find your positive spirit." Caleb stood up. "I will also help you to prepare for what is coming." He turned to walk out, the brown bag under his arm.

"Wait, wait!" I was after him as fast as I could. "This makes no sense!"

"It will, Deana Holliday. Do not let the evil take up residence in your heart. It is easily welcomed in, and difficult to dislodge." He was out the door before I could grab him or ask him anything more.

As he walked away, he shimmered, and then he was gone. What in the hell?

My first instinct was to call my aunts, but I needed to get through this one my own. They had enough going on without me pestering them at all hours.

But as I sat down at my desk, and went through the fairly common requests for PIs, I had to wonder just what in the hell I'd signed myself up for without even knowing it.

In his own way, Caleb was as scary as the vampires.

Jeez, this wasn't a good week for me to keep from being eaten. One way or the other—I was surrounded by man eaters. How in the hell would I get out this intact and alive?

CHAPTER SIX

THE REST OF MY DAY WAS BORING. FOR WHICH I THANKED whatever spirits might be lurking around, because I couldn't take any more excitement like the first two hours. I closed up, and went home to wait for Tuesday to wake up.

I hoped she'd managed to set up a date for us to meet this Alfonso Delgado, who seemed to be at the root of Kel's troubles. He was the guy who had sentenced him, he was the guy who'd refused to tell Kel why he was considered guilty, and I had to assume he was the guy who was keeping Lavina away from Kel.

That was a lot of shit rolled up into one ball of a man. None of which was good for me. Me being around would potentially throw a wrench into all the plans he had in motion, and the whole thing about how easily vampires could kill humans—I remembered Zachary's casual dismissal of such an event with a shudder—was never far from my thoughts.

Then I took a breath and stood up straight. I was in my closet, trying to decide what one wore to meet a killer vampire. I mean, one who killed for more than just food. They were hunters—so I needed to look like something other than prey.

Torn jeans, white tee shirt, several necklaces, including one my aunt Deirdre had given me before I went off to meet a necromancer, boots, and my leather jacket. A fire bag to help me cast a fire spell if I really needed to get the hell out there. I left the jacket on my bed and went down to eat. I wanted to be ready for whatever when Tuesday got up.

I was nearly finished eating when the sun had just set. Tuesday came into the kitchen so quietly that I didn't hear her, scaring the bejeesus out of me. "Oh!" I shouted, as she touched my shoulder. "You need to make more noise than that!"

Tuesday smiled. "You were lost in thought. I could have come in wearing bells, and I'm not sure you would have heard me."

I frowned. "It's been that kind of day. So what's up?"

"I know where Delgado will be tonight."

"Did you set up a meeting with him?"

"No. We will go to his club, and he will be unable to resist meeting you."

"Why?" I asked, afraid of the answer.

"Because he knows how I feel about him. And because there is something about you that will draw him in."

"Which is?"

"I told you, there is something in your past that is intriguing. I would love to see your family tree. He will be intrigued, as I am, which will be increased because you are with me, who is his sworn enemy."

"Is it safe for you to go there?"

"I have not been banned, and he is secure enough in his position to not worry. But he will be unable to keep his mouth shut," Tuesday grinned. "Very full of himself, is Delgado."

"No fighting, though, right?"

She shook her head. "You won't be the only human there. So no, no fighting."

"Okay, when do we leave?"

"I must make a few more calls, and then if you're ready, we'll go." She glided out the kitchen as silently as she'd entered, and I went upstairs to do some last minute primping to complete my bad ass image. And to tuck a few of the fire tea bags in my pockets; I was pretty sure vampires didn't care for fire.

When I came downstairs, Tuesday was waiting. She was dressed in a pair of white jeans, and a yellow golden shirt, which only made her look more fairy-like.

"Do you have a car?" I asked. I hadn't thought to ask last night, and wondered how she'd gotten here.

She shook her head.

"Then how do you feel about motorcycles?"

"That will be fine," she said.

A few moments later, we were heading out of Venice and towards Los Angeles. Tuesday told me the bar was near Santee Alley in the Fashion District. We parked outside of a building that looked completely derelict.

"Really?" I asked quietly. "Here?"

She nodded. "If you weren't with me, you wouldn't even notice it. Well," Tuesday turned to look at me with a tiny smile, "Maybe you would, Deana melting pot Holliday."

I was going to push Caleb to find out what I was. This was getting irritating.

Tuesday stepped in front of me and knocked on the door. After a moment, it opened, and she walked in. I followed, feeling my heart speed up. The door slammed behind me and I steeled myself not to jump.

"Why are you here?" A crisp, cold voice asked.

"Because I wanted to go out and am tired of pretending," she said, sounding bored.

A man stepped out of the shadow. He was tall, and thin with dark hair. He was the epitome of creeptastic, and had I seen him before the door closed, I might have run screaming, because holy hell. His skin was so pale it nearly glowed in the dark, and his eyes glittered like black beetles.

The whole effect was extremely unsettling.

"You're responsible for your guest," he said.

Tuesday nodded. He backed into the shadows again —where the hell did he go? And while I was trying to look without looking, Tuesday strode forward. I hurried to catch up. As I reached her side, she said, "Stay close. Don't look alarmed if I touch you. I need to make sure no one gets any ideas."

I was about to ask what she was talking about when I saw. She was right. I wasn't the only human here. I got the impression, however, that I had a completely different agenda than most of the other humans did. Mostly, I wasn't focused on getting laid, and there seemed to be a lot of that going around.

Tuesday kept walking toward the back, and stopped abruptly, sliding into a half-moon shaped booth.

"What now?" I whispered as I slid in next to her.

"Shhhh," she said.

I shushed. When a woman came over to take a drink order, moving faster than a normal human would, I ordered a Sapphire and tonic. Tuesday just nodded, and the waitress zipped away. I guess in here, they didn't feel like they had to hide. But it was disconcerting to my eyes.

"Let me do most of the talking," Tuesday whispered.

"What?" I asked.

Before she could answer, a man slid into the booth, next to her. "Tuesday, it is most... interesting to see you here," he said smoothly.

She stared at him like he was something on her shoe, and replied, "I didn't feel like pretending."

"Understandable," the man said. He patted her hand.

I could feel her revulsion from where I sat. I thought the man could as well, which was why he did it. Interesting, as he'd said.

"And who is your charming companion?" The man gazed at me, seemingly delighted, as though the tension wasn't ten feet thick at this table.

"I'm Deana Holliday," I said.

His eyebrows went up. "Holliday? As in the gunfighter?"

"Distant relation," I said, offering up a silent apology to my many times great-grandfather. No one would understand. And the connection wasn't known, which seemed like a better idea for everyone involved.

"Charming. I am Alfonso Delgado, the proprietor of this establishment. Welcome. It is your first time, yes?"

Delgado had the slightest accent, the merest hint. He sounded as though he'd originally come from South America. It was like honey in the ears.

I felt a kick on my ankle. Oh. It was honey on the ears. And it was deliberate. Apparently vampires could add a little glam to their words, to make you think what they wanted you to.

"It is," I smiled. "Thank you for the kind welcome."

He smiled. It was nearly genuine. His fangs gleamed in the low light. A shudder ran through me. This was a killer. Not just for food, but for fun. Power. Revenge. I remembered that Tuesday said he killed her partner. He did. I could feel it. And he was loving the fact that he knew Tuesday wanted to kick his ass, and wouldn't, for whatever vampy reasons.

"I am glad to hear it. What do you think?"

"It's definitely new to me," I said honestly.

"Then please enjoy, although I must warn you, this is a place where we feel comfortable. I ask that you respect that," his voice hardened.

"Of course," I said. "Actually, I wanted to meet you. I asked Tuesday to bring me here, and she was kind enough to do so."

"Yes?"

"Yes," I said. At that moment, the waitress came back with our drinks, and I took a sip, feeling calmer. This was known territory. I was looking for answers.

"Go on," Delgado said. His eyes had narrowed, even as he kept his smile in place.

"What is it that makes you think Kel Worthington killed Jessamine Cassidy?"

Delgado blinked, and then turned his head toward Tuesday. "This is why you brought her here?"

Tuesday shrugged, looking completely unconcerned about the menace in Delgado's tone. "Yes. She asked for my help and I was disposed to give it."

"I'm sure," Delgado said. Then he looked at me. "Why is this your interest, Miss Holliday?"

"I'm friends with Kel. He didn't know who else to ask."

He nodded, thinking. "I could kill you for your impertinence in coming here, questioning me. You, also," he said to Tuesday.

She smiled, a wide, fangy grin. "You could try."

He made a dismissive noise, and focused on me again. "But I'm in a good mood, so I shall answer you. First, Lavina is well-known for her temper. She was very upset with Jessamine."

"Why?" I asked.

"She has not chosen to share, to her detriment. But she is still upset, and it's not merely because Jessamine met the final death. Second, the human is very taken with her. It wouldn't be difficult to suggest to him to do this thing for Lavina." Now he did snort.

"Except he says he didn't. What is Lavina saying?"

"That she was upset, but that she wouldn't kill another of us, personally or by proxy."

"Why isn't her word good enough?"

At that, Delgado looked at me. "We have our reasons for doubting both Lavina and her human."

"Like you did with Sasha?" Tuesday's voice was cold enough to freeze the room.

"Sasha—oh, Tuesday. Why are you continuing to pine for Sasha? She is gone. I'd hoped, when I saw you with the most entrancing Miss Holliday, you'd taken the first steps forward. To the future," he said encouragingly, like he was a fucking life coach.

Tuesday didn't move. She didn't speak, blink, or even breathe. But I felt certain that if anyone moved even an eyelash, she'd have Delgado on his ass. In pieces. The air was that heavy with the promise of glorious revenge.

"Deana is a friend. That is all. Unlike you, I have them. And occasionally, I help them." Her voice was calm, and steady. But it was as though she held a sword over Delgado's head.

To which he was impervious, or really, really good at ignoring.

"That is a good thing, Tuesday. But I should tell you, I do not think you will be successful in determining Mr. Worthington's innocence. In frank terms," Delgado turned to me, threading his hands together in front of him on the table and maintaining the life-coach-you'd-like-to-kill-for-the-perkiness-alone persona, "Lavina is very strong. Not as strong as Jessamine, nor as skilled. Which is a fact that I believe may have had something to do with this conflict. Regardless, your human friend is very much in thrall to Lavina. It happens," he waved his hand casually. "Humans have a difficult time resisting us to begin with, and when the vampire is equally attracted... well," he shrugged. "Things happen. Neither party is thinking logically. All it would have taken is a suggestion."

"Would Kel remember the things he'd done while he was... in thrall?" I spoke carefully. I'd have to look that shit up when I got home. It sounded horrific. Like, something you kept secret.

Delgado hooted with laughter. "It's not like a light switch, Miss Holliday! You do not turn it on and off at a whim. It is something, a feeling, an urge, that builds the longer the vampire and human are involved. This one has lasted longer with Lavina than any she's been with in some time."

"So he would remember?" I pressed the point.

Delgado's laughter faded as though it had never been there. "He should, as a general rule. But there are no hard and fast rules when it comes to relationships. Have you ever been in love, Miss Holliday?"

How had I thought his voice mocking, or that he was a major douche canoe with a death wish? He was the most charming sounding man I'd ever met—

A second sharp kick at my ankle jerked me out of whatever mojo it was Delgado was laying on me. "Knock it off," I said, giving some stink eye of my own. "I'm very appreciative you've been willing to chat with me, but that is not a license to try and drag me off to the harem or whatever woo woo shit it is you're doing."

Delgado stared. Tuesday stared. The two male vamps near the table stopped pretending to ignore us and stared.

"Are you unfamiliar with manners, Miss Holliday?" The woo woo and warmth was completely gone from Delgado's voice.

"I can ask the same thing, Mr. Delgado. I'm here as

an act of faith, that I can come to you seeking information, and not be distracted with whatever game you're
attempting to play. This is not the way to manage a
budding relationship."

His eyebrow disappeared into his dark, carefully
arranged hair that fell just so across his forehead. "Is
this a budding relationship?"

"I view all my interactions as such. It makes the
world a much better place." I felt Tuesday's boot on my
foot. I slid it out from under her boot, and kept my eyes
on Delgado.

He stared at me so long I thought I was doomed for
a midnight snack, but then he smiled. "I must say I
agree with you. Tell me, Miss Holliday, what are your
origins?"

I thought I knew what he was asking, and while it
might be a risk, I took it. "My aunts live in Deadwood
and have for some time."

He nodded. "That makes sense. I have crossed paths
with them in the past, and they are honorable women. I
will allow for you to be the same."

"I am," I said. "Kel Worthington is someone I used
to be good friends with. We are no longer close, and
that is by choice. But if he's going to die, he deserves to
understand why." I figured it wouldn't get me anywhere
to argue this was unfair and rigged as hell. And remembering Zachary's very blasé attitude about humans
dying, I took a chance that Alfonso Delgado shared a
similar point of view.

He sighed. "I suppose so. But they die so easily, it gets tiresome keeping up with it all."

Now it was my eyebrow's turn to raise.

"Oh, very well, Miss Holliday. May I call you Deana? I feel we've become friendly enough for that. And you may call me Alfonso. I will also tell you that anytime you find yourself interested in my harem, or any such thing, all you need to do is let me know."

I felt the woo woo wash over me for a moment, and then it was gone. He was all business again. "Jessamine was staying with her mate in a house near the beach. They spend most of their time in the dust bowl of the desert, so Levi arranged to take a house to allow her to be near the water. She was very involved, as she always is, in scrying, and working her magic. She was happy to be a vampire with Levi, but witchcraft was her passion." He sighed. "She was the most amazing vampire I've ever known."

"Really?" I asked. It almost sounded as though he cared for her.

"Yes. I would have taken her into my clan, my harem," he winked at me, "In a flash, if she wished it. But she loved that crusted old man, that cowboy. And there was never another for her. So I merely flirted enough to annoy her mate, and admired her from afar."

"How do we know you're telling the truth?" Tuesday asked.

"You don't. But I find that I like the boldness of Deana, and have nothing to lose by being honest."

They stared at one another. I was going to get that story out of Tuesday if it killed me. You know, because I'm all about taking risks with vampires. I stifled a laugh to myself.

Delgado's head whipped to me. "Yes?"

"I'm sorry, Alfonso. I'm a little giddy at my own ball-syness. I knew I was walking into a den of predators, and yet, there's knowing, and then... knowing," I said, putting emphasis on the last word. "It's getting to me."

"Deana, you are lovely. You are also welcome here. As long as you mind your manners, and do not bother my guests. You may even bring your friend Tuesday. But you will not interfere in my business again. Is that understood?"

"Absolutely. One last thing, Alfonso," I smiled, just a small one, not gushing or anything. "Is it possible to talk to Lavina?"

Oh, shit. Now I'd done it. The silence around me suggested I'd gone too far. In for a penny, in for a pound. I smiled a bit more and waited.

"You have accused me of turning on the woo woo, but I think it's you who have the woo woo," Delgado said. "Or else I'm going insane. Yes, you may speak with Lavina. Take her," he said to one of the hovering males. "And Tuesday. They can have five minutes with Lavina, and then I'd suggest heading home for the evening." He stared to make sure his meaning was clear.

"Of course," I inclined my head, feeling like I was finally making some progress. "You are too kind."

"I am. Don't forget it," he said shortly as he stood and walked away. One of the males turned to walk with him, and the other waited for us.

As we got up and followed the second male into the back of the bar, I wondered how we were going to be leaving.

Hopefully upright and under our own steam.

CHAPTER SEVEN

"I'M NOT SURE IF YOU'RE STUPID OR A GENIUS," TUESDAY hissed.

I opened my mouth to respond and she made a shushing motion, gesturing at Delgado's guy in front of us. Nodding, I shut my mouth. There would be plenty of time to talk later. Like when we made it out of here safely. I wasn't fooled by Delgado's show of tolerance and amusement. He'd kill us the moment it became to his advantage.

But right now, I was trying to keep Kel alive. I'd deal with Delgado looking for a favor in return later.

The guy in front of us led us down a small hallway at the back of the bar. He pushed open a door, and stood to the side, waiting for us to enter. "You have five minutes," his voice was deep.

I started to walk in but an iron bar in the form of

Tuesday's arm stopped me. "I'll go first," she said. She pushed past me, and I followed, a little unnerved.

A sudden movement had Tuesday pushing me back out the door. I heard her hiss something and I stepped back into the shadow of the hallway.

More hissing and then I heard Tuesday again. "You can come in, Deana."

Stepping in cautiously, I saw that Tuesday had her arm around another blond woman. But where Tuesday looked like a fairy tale come to life, this woman was Barbie on steroids. She had long, wavy blond hair, and her eyes were fierce.

At the moment, she wasn't smiling.

"I'm Deana Holliday," I said.

"You're a friend of Kel's."

"We were friends," I said.

"He was a dick to you after Derek died," she said. "He told me about it, and I told him he was wrong."

"He was," I said shortly. I wasn't going to get into this now. "Listen, we only have a few minutes. Then we're going to have to leave. What happened with you and Jessamine?"

Her lips pursed together. "I don't—"

"I don't care what your issue is," I got closer to her. "If you care about Kel at all, you need to tell me what you know."

"I went to see Jessamine to get some herbs from her. She's—she was—really great at drying them so that they are still effective when you're ready to use them."

77

"You're a witch?" I asked.

"No. There are just certain herbs I use. For my own personal use." Her face took on a mulish expression.

"I don't care why you use them. What I'm trying to understand is why you were there, and what happened to Jessamine."

"She was alive when I left."

"Why did you argue?"

"Because she was scrying when I came in, and we argued over what she saw. She was still in the middle of her reading, and I overheard it. I told her she needed to come clean, to tell someone what she saw. She refused, said it wasn't her place to get involved."

"Involved in what?" Tuesday asked.

Lavina's lips pursed together again.

"Kel is going to die if you don't tell me what is going on," I said.

"Better than both of us dying. If I tell what I heard now, it won't do a damn thing for me."

"But it's all cool if Kel dies?" I asked angrily.

"No!" she burst out. "No! I don't want him to die. But I can't save him—why do you think they have me locked up in here? Because I'd find him and run away and tell all these assholes," she raised her voice, no doubt to let the guy in the hallway hear her, "To piss off!" She glared at the doorway.

No one came in, so I guessed they were used to hearing her cuss them out. I just stared at her. All this anger was well and good, but it wasn't getting us any—

Lavina gestured to me, beckoning me closer. "Listen, Jessamine wrote it down. If you can get her diary, she has what she saw written down. I thought she was crazy, but she just might be the genius that saves me and Kel. Go to her house and look in the room she was using as a workroom. The diary will be in there." She spoked in a hurried whisper.

"Unless her mate has already cleared her things," Tuesday said.

"This soon? Please," Lavina rolled her eyes to show her thoughts on the mate taking such an action. "It has to be found and shared by someone other than me. No one will believe me, and all it will get me is being left in the sun somewhere the minute it comes out. You know," she looked at Tuesday. "You know that Jessamine usually got it right when she scried. I have no reason to think she'd break the streak now."

"Do you have any idea who killed her?" I asked. This was all very interesting, but it wasn't helping Kel.

"If her scrying that night was known, yes, I would think who killed her would be obvious. I don't think it is, though, so I really don't have any idea."

Delgado's man opened the door. "Your time is up."

"Tell Kel I love him," said Lavina. She sounded like she meant it.

"I will," I said.

The man showed us to a door, and when we walked outside, slammed it shut behind us with force.

"Let's get out of here," Tuesday muttered.

We found my bike and headed home, neither of us speaking. Once we'd gotten safely inside the house, Tuesday sat down in the kitchen and looked at me. "You're very lucky," she said.

"What? Because of Delgado? He's the kind of guy who thinks of us like pets, doesn't he?"

She looked surprised, and then approving. "Yes, he is. Most humans don't figure that out until it's too late."

I rolled my eyes. "His kind are a dime a dozen."

"That is where you are wrong. He may seem charming in the worst sort of sleazy way, but he is dangerous. You are on his radar now. He likes the idea of you, finds you intriguing. He will not forget you, and he's the kind of person you want to forget you."

I sat down, sighing. "Life was a lot simpler, a lot less deadly, before I knew I was a witch."

"You didn't know?"

"My great grannie left Deadwood and didn't speak of it fondly. She never went back. We had no idea how witchy," I didn't have a better word, "Their lives are. And I didn't know that everyone and their monster brother knew them."

Tuesday laughed. "They are very serious about their mission."

"Don't I know it. But even as easy as it is to trade on the family name, I figure there's a cost involved."

"There is." The laughter was gone from Tuesday's face.

"Yeah, well, one more thing to worry about later. It's

not like I can change who my family is. And it's not like I can change the past, which everyone always seems aware of," I was referring to the recent dustup with the demon in Deadwood.

"Better to use it for your advantage."

"What happened with your partner? Sasha?" I asked.

She looked at me, and then looked away. "She argued with Delgado. Told him that we didn't have a king, so he could quit pretending. Three nights later, I found her body."

"Oh, no," I said.

"Not her head. Just her body. With her jewelry, and all the things that I knew were hers. He killed her, but he did it in a way where there is no absolute proof that she's actually dead, and that he is not tied to in any way."

"I believe you," I said.

"That's kind. No one else does. Or rather, they are taking the easy way out Delgado offered them. No head, no positive ID, and therefore, no one has to make him answer for anything." Her voice was bitter.

"I'm sorry," I said.

"I miss her and will until the day I meet the final death," Tuesday said. "But that doesn't solve our concern at the moment."

"How the hell are we going to get Jessamine's diary?" I asked.

"*IF* Lavina is telling the truth."

"Did she seem like she was lying to you?"

Tuesday looked at me like I'd grown another head. "Really?"

"That was a serious question. I couldn't tell if she was lying. She seemed sincere, in that 'I've resigned myself to my fate as long as I don't die,' sort of way."

Tuesday smiled. "She does seem rather self-absorbed, doesn't she?"

"Why wouldn't she just tell the truth about what Jessamine saw?"

Tuesday shrugged. "That, I don't know."

"We have to get that diary."

"That will be far easier said than done. Her mate will be on high alert, and he's going to attack first, then ask questions. That's if he's in the mood to talk at all." Her voice was dark.

"Do you have a better idea?" I asked.

She looked away, and then sighed. "No."

"Then let's find a way to get him out of the house so we can run in and grab the diary."

"What's the we business? You think you're going with me? You're as slow as a drunken elephant, and just as noisy," Tuesday was scathing.

"I can drive the getaway bike, then," I said. There was no way I was being left out on this one. Or anything. This was my case, and I would be there for all things connected. Good or ill.

She sighed again. "You are really very persistent. It makes things difficult."

"I work for my clients. Why can't we just call him, talk, be out in the open? Or is that not how vampires work?" I asked.

"I suppose you want to do this tonight?"

"Kel is down to less than five days," I said.

"All right. Let me consider for a bit. I need fifteen minutes." She strode off to where she was sleeping, leaving me in the kitchen.

All in all, Tuesday was all right. The rest? I shuddered a little, thinking about both Zachary and Alfonso. I decided I'd take my crazy witch family over all this vampire drama any day of the week. At least my aunts just yelled at you when they were not happy.

Although since there was major drama surrounding all the secrets that were coming out about my family, maybe I shouldn't cast stones, or roll my eyes too hard. I couldn't complain. Tuesday had been incredibly helpful every step of the way—I had no reason to think she'd change tactics now.

At least, I hoped not.

While I contemplated if I'd make it through to the morning, Tuesday came out. "All right. I'm ready. Let's go. I'll tell you what we're doing when we get there."

"Why not now? Before we leave, and venture into the dangerous, stressful situation with the vampire whose all mad with grief?"

"Because I don't want to hear any shit from you about the plan," Tuesday said, heading for the garage.

I followed her out for the second time that night.

At some point, I needed to take back control of this growing circus. But maybe not right this second.

CHAPTER EIGHT

TUESDAY HAD PUT THE ADDRESS INTO MY PHONE, AND I drove up the Pacific Coast Highway toward Malibu. The address was in a swanky beach community right near Point Dume. Driving the Chief up the highway at night was amazing, and for a moment, I forgot that I was on a quest to play hide and seek with a vampire.

A pissed off, grieving, not-in-the-mood vampire, no doubt. But who's worrying? I smiled despite the tension, because there is nothing better than winding up the coast on your bike. Nothing.

Nope, not even that.

All too soon, I was turning off the PCH onto the road that led out toward the point. When the map showed that we were there, I drove past the house, and parked further down the street. There really wasn't anywhere to park, which made me even more glad I'd brought the bike. My Land Cruiser would have stuck out like a sore thumb.

"Be quiet," Tuesday whispered even though I hadn't said a word. "I'm going to call him and tell him that I have heard something about Jessamine's death—that I spoke with Lavina."

"You're going to tell him the truth?" I didn't think this was in the plan.

"Easier. I'll ask him to meet me, and when he leaves, we'll go in and find the diary."

"That's the big plan?"

"You have a better idea?"

I considered. "No. It gets him out of the house."

"Exactly. Now be quiet." She dialed a number into her phone and talked quietly.

Vampires seemed to do everything fast. She talked in a low tone, and she was speaking quickly, so I couldn't really understand.

"We need to stay out of sight," Tuesday said.

Together, we crouched down behind the Chief, and waited. We didn't have to wait long. Within five minutes, a car sped out of the circular driveway in front of the house. When the brake lights disappeared around the turn to the main road, Tuesday stood up. "Let's go."

"I get to come in with you now?"

"Better than leaving you out here," she said over her shoulder.

We hurried to the door, and Tuesday fiddled with

the lock. Normally, I would have done this, because hello? Lock pick skills right here, but I was happy to let her take the lead. Within moments, the lock clicked and the door opened.

We stepped in, and Tuesday took a deep breath.

"This way," she said.

"How can you tell?"

"Lavina said she came here for herbs. That means a stillroom of some kind, and it's very fragrant."

The house wasn't big, and as we stepped into a room, I flicked on the light. It was like stepping into a medieval movie. There were drying racks with various herbs and flowers hanging off it, and there were lines strung across the room with more bundles of herbs and plants tied together hanging off the line.

It was charming.

"Okay, where would she keep it?" I prowled around, looking at the table of things that Jessamine had left. She wasn't tidy, but I would bet she'd known where everything was. It was a chaotic kind of order.

I found a small, leather bound book among a stack of papers. "I think this is it," I said. Flipping it open, I went to the last page where there was writing.

"Shit." The one word echoed through the room.

"What?"

I looked up. "It's in code," I said. "Can you read this?"

Tuesday came over and took the book. She thumbed through the pages, her eyes scanning. "No," she said as she shook her head. "This must be her own personal code. I don't understand it."

"You're not meant to," a deep, masculine voice said from behind us.

I stopped, and lowered my hands, one reaching into my pocket for a fire bag. I said the spell in my head a few times, ready to cast it. I couldn't see what Tuesday was doing because she was off to my side and I was staring straight ahead, barely daring to breathe.

"Set down the journal, and turn around," the man commanded.

Doing as he asked, I saw that Tuesday put the book back onto the table. We both looked up at the guy who'd caught us, and I took a breath.

Wow.

This really wasn't the right time, but I couldn't help but admire him. He had salt-and-pepper gray hair, and his face was tan. He must have been in his forties when he turned, because he didn't have the overly youthful face of some of the vampires I'd seen so far. He also had a mustache like you read about in an old West novel—big, bushy, and while I wasn't a fan of mustaches, it looked absolutely fantastic on him.

He was dressed all in black, and all he needed was a cowboy hat and a horse to be ready to ride off into the sunset a hundred years ago.

He was gorgeous. His voice was gorgeous. I supposed if I was about to die, this wouldn't be a bad thing to see right before I rolled on out.

"I know you, Tuesday Galloway. I do not know the human with you. Nor do I know what the two of you are doing in my home, looking through the things of my mate."

"Trying to find her killer," I said.

I felt Tuesday's glare.

"Her killer has been found."

"Not according to him. And not according to his girlfriend, who supposedly sent him to do this."

"What will you do?" Tuesday asked.

"Well, my first instinct is to just kill you, be done with it. I don't need any more things to manage," he said. "But if you're here, Tuesday Galloway, you must feel there is a reason to be so. Maybe I'll wait a bit, see what you have to say. Before I decide whether I'm going to kill you."

"That would be really great. The not killing thing, I mean," I burst out before I could stop myself.

Tuesday rolled her eyes and made a sound that could only be described as disgusted.

"I'm Levi Cassidy. You are?"

"Deana Holliday."

"Holliday?"

"Fourth cousin," I said. Even before I knew about my Deadwood family, I got this reaction a lot. It was kind of funny that it even happened with a vampire and then the thought struck me—he might have known Doc. Probably not the best time to ask.

Levi nodded. "Come into the living room. Bring the

journal," he added, looking at us both. "I can read it, if you give me a good reason as to why I should." He turned on his heel, clearly expecting us to hop to it.

And clearly not afraid of having us at his back. For some reason, that scared me more than anything else had tonight. I'm a confident gal—and I don't turn my back on anyone.

Levi moved smoothly through the dark rooms of his house. I kept close to Tuesday because why couldn't these damn vampires turn on a light? If I wasn't worried about falling on my face, my eyes would be rolling to the next state.

Thankfully, he turned a light on once we reached a room with large glass doors. The moon was bright out over the ocean. I could see why Jessamine wanted to be here, even if she couldn't enjoy it during the day.

Levi rounded on us. "Why are you here? Tell me the truth."

Tuesday sighed.

I stepped forward, hand out, before she could say anything. "I'm Deana Holliday, as I told you. I run an investigative agency. Kel, the man accused of killing Jessamine, is an old friend of mine. He asked for my help. The only reason I've been able to find out anything is because of my aunts—you may know them? The Nightingales of Deadwood?" I handed him the diary—or journal, as he referred to it.

Levi's eyebrows went up as he took the journal back from me—they were dark black, and gave him an air of authority, mixed in with his salt and pepper hair—I stopped myself. I really needed to focus on something other than the fact that I found him extremely attractive. Because you know, the whole killing thing.

"I know the Nightingales." He looked at me. "But I do not know you."

"My great gran is the fourth sister. She left Deadwood."

Levi shook his head. "Humans are odd. Be that as it may, you are not your aunts. So why, if you're working for the man who killed my mate, should I believe anything you say?"

"Because I don't want him to die, even if he is kind of a dickhead, and I hate seeing the wrong person pay for a crime," I said, surprising myself. I didn't mean to tell Levi this much, but the words kept falling out of my mouth.

He nodded as if in understanding. "That might be a waste of your time, but it's not a bad thing to want to see right done." Levi sat down. "Sit. Neither of you is going anywhere anytime soon. Tell me why you want Jessamine's journal."

I looked at Tuesday.

"This is your show, Deana. For the record, I was against this," she directed that last bit at Levi.

"Thanks," I said. Some ally.

"Why do you need it?" Levi asked.

I sighed. "All right. So we went to talk to Alfonso Delgado," I noted that Levi's lip came up in a sneer,

"And he has Lavina, the vampire who argued with your mate, locked away for the foreseeable future. We got to see her, but—"

"How did you manage that?" Levi asked.

"There is a leprechaun on her person," Tuesday said dryly.

Levi nodded. I felt like there was a lot being said that I wasn't understanding, but I wasn't in a place to pick that apart.

"Go on," he said.

"Lavina said she came here to get some herbs from Jessamine, and that Jessamine was scrying, and wasn't quite done. Lavina heard some of what Jessamine said… and that's what they argued over. Lavina said she told Jessamine she had to share whatever it was she saw, and Jessamine said no, and," I shrugged, "That's what they argued about."

"What did Jess see?"

"Lavina wouldn't share that," Tuesday interjected. "Whatever it was, it scared her. She said she wasn't the person to share the information—that she'd be killed as soon as it was known. She's afraid. That, she is not lying about."

"What do you think she's lying about?" I asked.

Now it was Tuesday's turn to shrug. "I don't know. I know that Lavina is, as we've discussed, very interested in self-preservation."

"As are all of us," Levi said quietly. He was looking at

the small leather book in his hands. "I can read her code. I can tell you what it was she saw."

"How do we know which prophecy or whatever it was?" I asked.

"She did not work again before she was killed," Levi said. "I left for business the next evening, and Jess was on the beach. She had no plans to work." Before, he'd looked middle-aged. Now, he looked very old, and tired. And sad.

"I'm sorry," I said.

His head shot up. "Thank you. I'm still... well, we were together for a long time. I find that I am still looking for her. I was looking forward to seeing your friend pay for his act, but if he is not the one who did this, the real killer must be found."

"Kind of the point," I replied. "Are you willing to read the last entry to us, then? See what it is she saw that started all of this?"

He stared at me, and I wondered if I'd gone too far. I was doing a lot of wondering in that realm this week, and I felt like perhaps I was pushing my luck, but I also got the feeling that vampires respected strength. They were predators. If you showed fear, you went right into the 'prey' category.

And I was no one's prey.

"Yes, I will."

I pulled out my phone, ready to record him. Levi turned the pages of the book, his fingers brushing lightly over the pages, almost reverently.

"Here it is," he said. "Give me a moment. It's been some time since I read her work."

We waited silently, watching Levi as he read through the journal. Finally, after what seemed an eternity, he looked up, and leaned back.

"I can see why Jess didn't want to share this," he said slowly. "It would have been a death sentence."

"What is it?" I asked, trying not to reach over and shake him.

"She was filling a scry request for..." He stopped. "For Delgado."

"I knew his hand was in this," Tuesday muttered.

"What did she see?"

"This is what it says. 'The spells made will backfire. The merger of dem and del will fail, but not before dragging everyone down. Consider how to share. Must be diplomatic.'" Levi stopped.

"And?" I asked. "Was she writing in some kind of shorthand?" What was dem and del? Del was Delgado. I'd bet the Chief on it.

"That's it, and yes, she did use her own sort of shorthand."

"Didn't Lavina say that Jessamine also did spell work?" I was trying to remember who had said it—and failing.

Levi nodded. "She was gifted."

"So who was her last spell client?"

"That, I don't know," he set the book down next to him.

"Something for Delgado?" Tuesday asked.

"We could ask—" I began, as Tuesday skewered me with a glare.

"No, we could not ask." Her voice brooked no discussion.

"I could," Levi said. "I could inquire if she finished the work for him."

"What, you're on the team now?" I shook my head. "You guys go from 'oh, let's kill you' to 'Yeah, let's work together' awfully quick." I couldn't deny that the thought of working with him made my heart speed up, and I wondered what my two vampire companions made of that? Let them think I'm annoyed.

"It's one of the benefits of being extremely practical," Levi said.

"Don't ask him. If this is what Lavina and Jessamine both felt was killing information, better that he not know we have it." This was one thing I was sure about. No need to update Delgado on anything.

"So what do you plan to do?" Levi looked at me.

So did Tuesday.

"I don't know. Honestly, it's been a long night, and I'm in a bit of info overload. Can you keep that safe?" I nodded at the journal. "Like, lock and key safe. I need to go home and sleep and think. And unlike you two, I have to go into work tomorrow."

"Then we should leave. I am sorry we broke in," Tuesday said to Levi, oddly formal.

"It was practical," I couldn't resist.

Tuesday didn't look at me, but Levi smiled, just the corners of his mouth turning up as he stood. "I can see where you'd think so," he said. "I'll show you out the door this time."

I kept my mouth shut and nodded. He didn't need to know that we'd picked the lock. He might already know. I wasn't going to worry about it.

What I needed now was to get home and get to sleep and try not to drift off on the way home.

Tired as I was, I saw Levi's little smile all the way home.

CHAPTER NINE

MY ALARM NEEDED TO DIE. IT WAS GOING OFF IN THE most annoying fashion, and all I wanted was to go back to bed. I slapped in the general direction of where it was yelling at me but missed. It kept yelling. Finally, I got up, and hauled myself to the shower.

After three cups of coffee, I crawled into Baby, my FJ cruiser (no Chief today), and made it to my office in time to open the door and make a pot of coffee just in time for opening. And just when I wanted to sit at my desk and close my eyes, the bell over the door jangled.

"Hi, how can I help you?" I asked as I got up. The glare from the sun blinded me for a moment and I couldn't see anything more than an outline.

Then he stepped forward. He was tall, and thin, and looked young. His hair stood up in messy spikes, but it was deliberate, because everything about this man was deliberate. He wore a suit, and wow, did it look good on him.

There was something more about him. Which led me to wonder if there was some sort of mark on my place—because my supernatural/other clients were outnumbering the work I had to do on what I was calling my 'normals.'

"Hello," he said, holding out a hand. "I'm Madigan."

I took his hand. "Deana Holliday. How can I help you?"

Madigan sat down without me even saying anything. "Let's be honest, Ms. Holliday. I know who your family is, and you have, no doubt, by now figured out that I'm not just another guy in a suit."

Putting my desk between us, I sat down and gave him my best stink eye. "I got that impression."

He nodded, smiling pleasantly. "Excellent. Saves time when all parties are... out in the open."

"What are you?"

"I beg your pardon?" His smile never shifted.

Creepy. In a kind of... attractive way. What was wrong with me?

"What are you? You know my back story. I'm asking for information."

"Well, let's say, I'm extended family of the... gentleman you and your aunts sent to Hell recently."

Whatever I'd been expecting, that wasn't it. "I'm sorry? You're related to... no. You look...nothing alike."

He laughed, sounding genuinely pleased. "No, some

of us go for a more modern look, but there are always people who prefer a more traditional life."

Yeah, I guess you'd call Ashlar's horns and gross loincloth 'traditional' in demon-land. "If you say so," I said.

"Well, it takes all types. Anyway, I'm not here because of that, although I won't deny it piqued my interest."

"Great," I said, not even trying to keep my disgust hidden.

"Patience, Ms. Holliday. I'm here on business, business for myself. I would like you to find something for me."

"Oh?"

"I'm looking for a pistol. A Volcanic pistol made around the time of the Civil War," he said, leaning back in his chair and gazing at the ceiling with his hands clasped in front of him.

"You're going to have to give me more than that," I said, opening my laptop and starting a file. "Any Volcanic? A particular serial number? Did it belong to someone in particular? How many were made?"

"This is a particular pistol. It's enchanted. I don't need some Civil War weapon that might blow my hand off in the normal course of things," he said, leaning forward and looking earnestly at me.

How the hell did he look like such a good guy? I found that despite his family connections, I liked him. I liked the direct manner he took with me.

But then I remembered. This was a demon, and given what my family was still going through, they were tricky as shit. Maybe this guy had found that his earnest businessman in a suit served him better. Better to assume he was up to something that would blow up in my face.

Wait. I didn't have to take his business. I straightened my shoulders. "I'm really sorry, Mr. Madigan, but I won't be able to help you."

"No?" He still smiled pleasantly.

"No," I shook my head. "I'm actually booked pretty solid for the foreseeable future, and I wouldn't want to take on a case that I wasn't able to give the proper attention to."

"Deana—may I call you Deana?"

I nodded. Here comes the knife, I thought.

"You're probably the only person who can find this for me. I'm not going to ask you to actively look for it, but if it should come into your hands, you are to call me immediately. I will make this financially lucrative for you, of course."

"I'm really sorry, but I am not taking this case." I stood up, pasting on my own pleasant fake smile.

"Sit down, please."

I remained standing.

He sighed. "Well, have it your way." He stood, brushing off the tops of his pants. "I'll make this simple. When you come across the Volcanic, you will let me know, and you will turn it over to me. Is that clear?"

"Perhaps you didn't hear me the first two times. I am not taking the case."

"And you are not listening to me. I am not asking," he said. "If you do not have it for me, in say, the next month or so, I will take it out on," he waved his hand around, "Your nice, new business."

"What?" He was clearly psycho.

"Oh, don't worry. I won't shut you down completely. But it will make it difficult with the full schedule you currently have."

I didn't know what to say.

"Thank you for your time, Deana. I look forward to seeing you sooner rather than later and concluding our business. Have a pleasant afternoon." He strolled out the door like he didn't have a care in the world.

I sat back down. Like I didn't have enough shit going on? Then I opened my laptop and looked up Volcanic pistols. They were an early pistol made by a company that folded into the Winchester company right after the Civil War.

Well, at least now I knew what I was looking at if it should come across my path. Madigan had spoken as though he was sure it would. And it was enchanted? I shook my head. I wanted to dismiss it, but my meager experience with demons suggested that would be a seriously bad call.

There was no helping it. I had thirty days to prove no such thing would cross my path, my doorstep, or anywhere in my universe.

As much as his visit had unsettled me, I had to get to work. Kel had a little over three days left. And I still had no idea who had killed Jessamine.

The rest of the morning was spent catching up on my emails from other clients—lost sister, lost daughter, lost father, is my husband cheating—that sort of thing. Thankfully, most of this could be done online, but a few required me to head out and sit in the car. Today would be a great day for that.

I also put in a few calls to the local police department on behalf of Zachary's request. He was looking for someone who'd been stealing from members of his coven. Why he thought I'd be better at this, I didn't know, but I wanted to address it and get it off my plate.

I decided I'd head out after lunch, wanting to put as many of these cases to bed as I could. And I needed to call Kel. That one, I was dreading. I knew a lot more, but not enough to get him off the hook. Or keep him alive.

Lunch first. There was a place a few doors down from me that did the best cheeseburgers I'd ever eaten. It was a dive bar, but whoever it was they had in the kitchen made the perfect cheeseburger. Which was perfect for today.

I sat at the bar and had a tonic water while I waited. Once my order was ready, I went back to my office, and saw someone standing at the door. He turned around, and I saw that it was Caleb.

"Come in," I said, unlocking the door.

"I've interrupted your lunch," he said in his somber tone.

"Yes, but it doesn't mean you're unwelcome." I found that I liked him immensely. His story had been rattling around my head since I'd heard it—two days ago? Was that it? It was so sad, and yet, he didn't seem sad about dying.

"You look good today," I said.

"I am as I am every day."

I sat back at my desk. "Okay, tell me what it is you would like me to do after you die," I said. I was proud of myself for not wincing as I said the word.

"I didn't come here for that today."

"Oh?"

"Please eat," he gestured at my bag of burger.

I noted that the brown bag was under his arm again. It seemed like it was part of him.

"No. I have heard that you are trying to save a human from vampire justice."

"Is this from your message boards again?"

"Of course."

"I need to be on those boards."

"You can have my account," Caleb said.

"Is that what you want to give me?"

"Later," he shook his head. "That is something we will come to later. You have listened to my story. When a person hears the life of another, then there is no real death. I thank you," he said, inclining his head formally.

I set down the burger I was about to take a bite out of. "Caleb, this is making me nervous."

He smiled. "Think of this as hospice for the weird."

I laughed. "I feel bad even laughing at that."

"Laughter is not a bad thing. Laughing about the good in people, even if they are dying, is healthy. This way, you'll remember me well."

"Okay." I glanced at the burger, which was cooling by the second.

"Eat, Deana. I wanted to help you. I understand you're working with a vampire?"

I nodded, my mouth full.

"I don't know why she hasn't suggested it, probably because it's something they don't allow outsiders to know, but the way to prove what your friend did or didn't do is with his blood."

"What?" I didn't want to get into blood and vampires. It made me a little nervous.

"Have the lead vampire or whoever it is who is running this take a drop of his blood. If he's lying, they'll be able to see it."

"Why didn't they do that at first?" I dropped the cheeseburger, I was so pissed. All this running around? And bullshit?

"It must be freely given."

"Why didn't Lavina do this?"

Caleb shrugged. "She no doubt has things to hide."

"Jesus, Mary, and Joseph. All the effort I've been going to for this—" I pushed away from my desk. "I could kill every one of their fangy selves. They knew, all along."

"Not all vampires know," Caleb leaned forward. "It's not well known, and the heads of the covens keep it low key. Can you imagine? It would be a bloodbath."

I looked at him, and then we both burst out laughing. "More than usual, you mean?"

"I am sorry I didn't meet you earlier, Deana Holliday. I enjoy your company, and that isn't the case with most humans."

"Ah, but I'm not entirely human, remember? Speaking of which, what else am I?"

"Are you really that intent on knowing?"

"If one more person sniffs me like some creepy uncle and asks me what I am, all my normal good behavior is going to go right out the window."

He smiled. "Finish your burger. It's no doubt colder than it should be but finish it. Then we'll see." He got up and walked outside.

My life was getting weirder and weirder. However, just in case I forgot who I was, my phone rang, and it was my mom.

"Hey," I said, "I'm eating before this thing gets stone cold. What's up?"

"I'm calling you to ask the same thing. What's going on?" Mom had her worried voice on.

"What do you mean?"

"Don't try and stall, Deana Holliday! Some sort of shit is hitting the fan!" Mom sounded put out.

"How is it with the curse and demons and whatever up there?"

"It's going. That's all I'm going to say. It's going. But I woke up this morning worrying about you. What's going on?" she asked again.

"My cases are coming in fast and furious. I have normal stuff, and then I have stuff like the aunts would see," I said carefully.

"You're mixed up in something, aren't you?"

"Mom, are we more than just witches?"

"What?"

Well, at least I'd stopped the tirade that was building.

"Are we more than just witches?" I spoke clearly, having finished the burger.

"Why would you ask that?"

"Because the other people... you know, like us... they keep sniffing me and asking me what else I am."

"What are you asking me, Deana?"

"Um, I don't know. Who was my dad? My grandad? Great grandad? Somewhere in there is something that is setting off all the sniffers around me."

The bell rang as Caleb walked back in. He sat in front of the desk and set the bag under the chair.

"I don't know, Deana. None of us seemed to have much luck with men sticking around, and honestly, it seemed easier to let your dad go."

"Mom, I have to go. I have a client here."

"I'll ask your grandmother and see what the aunts

know. And then you're going to tell me everything, you got it?"

"Yes, ma'am," I said.

"Don't patronize me."

"I'm not. I have to go. Love you," I said.

"Love you, too, brat."

When I hung up, Caleb was smiling.

"What?"

"We're always children to our parents."

"Yes, we are. Now, you're sure about the blood thing? I can ask them to see via Kel's blood?"

He nodded. "They won't be happy you know, but promise them you'll keep it secret, and swear with your own blood, since that's something they hold sacred, and they'll let you go. Don't tell them where you found out, though. It's important they think you are just very good at your job."

"I don't share client info with other clients," I said.

"I didn't think you would. I'm just offering advice from my own experience."

"I appreciate it," I said. "I need to give you back the mon—"

"No, you do not. Remember what I said? I must give away my possessions. I do not have much more than I need to be comfortable, and fulfill my job, but I want to give it to you. I like you, Deana Holliday."

"I like you, too. I wish—"

"Do not wish that. It's my time."

"Can I be with you?"

"No, I am like a cat. I must go on my own. But I'm not dead yet, and there is more to do. Give me your hand."

I wiped my hands on the napkin I had on my desk and stretched my left hand across to him. He took it between his own. His hands were warm, and big. His touch made me feel safe, which was weird. His hands were rough, like he'd worked with them his whole life.

"Close your eyes."

"Why?"

"Because it's easier to do this without you gawking at me," Caleb shot back.

I closed my eyes. The warmth in his hands increased, and I could hear him humming a song with a tune that was unfamiliar, almost alien to me.

CHAPTER TEN

MY HAND IN CALEB'S WAS GETTING WARMER. I WONDERED if it would get so hot that it would burn. His song got louder, and I peeked for a moment. His eyes were closed, and he was swaying slightly. Worried that I'd get caught, I closed my eyes again.

When I peeked again, my hand and wrist was glowing. Like, a lightbulb went off in them. What in the actual hell?

Then Caleb dropped my hand, and the light went out. "Open your eyes," he said.

"What's the verdict?"

"You are a witch on your mother's side. You will be a very strong witch, if you allow yourself. Your father—he was human. He, too, was strong. I think one must be, to be with a Nightingale." He closed his eyes, inhaling deeply.

"Further than your father, though, there is something more. I cannot tell where it came from, but there is the something that everyone else can sense in you."

"What is it?"

He looked at me then, and his eyes were sad. "It is demon."

I shoved myself away from the desk. "There is no way in hell," I said.

"Well, I don't actually think it was in Hell—"

"This is no time to be funny!" I shouted. I got up, and walked to the back of the office, kicking the wall for good measure.

"I'm not," Caleb said. "I'm sorry to tell you that. But—"

I rounded on him. "There is no but! I've met exactly two demons in my life, and it's all been in the last month, and they have both been complete shitheads! And now you're telling me that I'm like that? I'm one of them?"

"Are you?" Caleb asked.

"Don't try to Yoda me, Caleb Black!"

Wisely, he kept his mouth shut as I paced up and down the small hallway that housed the bathroom and a back office. That's where I kept my files, my safe, and a futon. Not that I'd been able to use it today, when I really needed it. Nor did it look like I was going to.

When I came back into the front of the office, Caleb was standing. "I'm sorry to upset you. I'll come and see you again, when it's closer to my time. I am sorry,

Deana. If you want to talk about this, you have my number."

He picked up his ratty brown bag, and walked out the door, leaving me seething and looking for a fight.

THREE HOURS LATER, I hadn't found it. I had found the husband of one of my clients hanging out with a woman that was not my client in a manner that seemed far too up close and personal for a coworker. I took the pictures that she wanted and emailed her right then to let her know I had them. I sent an invoice as well. As soon as she paid, the pictures and the husband were her problem.

I didn't go back to the office. But I still needed to call Kel, and then go home to wait for my vampire sidekick —she'd kill me dead on the spot if I called her that out loud—and ask about the blood test.

I sighed. May as well call Kel now.

He answered on the first ring. "Dee-Deana! It's less than three days! What have you found out?"

"Oh, I've found out a lot, and I might have the key to saving your life. But I don't know yet, and I won't until tonight. So, stay where you are, and don't do anything dumb assed."

"But what—"

"I'm not going to talk about it until I know for sure. Oh, I saw Lavina last night."

"How is she?" His voice changed, to one of the eager lover boy.

I remembered what Delgado had said about being in thrall. He was in something, all right. "She said she's fine, but she's worried for you, and wants you to be careful. For her. She also said to tell you she loves you." I was embellishing a little, but if this whole blood thing was wrong, I didn't need him running around like a crazy person. If he thought Lavina was telling him to lay low, he might listen to her.

"Does she know you're helping me?"

I rolled my eyes. "She does, and she feels like you have a chance. But she said, more than once, Kel, that you can't do anything that might make things worse for you, or for her."

"Oh, god, they're going to hurt her, aren't they?"

"I don't think so. I think they're making sure she doesn't run off."

"She wanted to," his voice was morose now. "I said no, and now look."

"Well, listen to her, please. I'll call you tonight after I know more, okay? I promise. I'm not going to leave you hanging. I just can't give you an answer now."

"No matter how late?"

"It will probably be late. They keep late hours," I said, thinking about last night.

"Yeah, I know. But it was worth it," he sighed. "Call me, Dee."

I didn't even correct his use of the nickname he used to call me. "I will."

We hung up. I hoped like hell I'd have good news for him. Now all I needed to do was figure out how to talk a vampire in charge into taking a drop of his blood.

As I drove home, I realized I had about three hours until it was good and dark. Which was just enough time for a nap.

I was asleep as soon as my head hit the pillow.

I woke to someone shaking me. "Mom, stop! I'm not late."

"I'm not your mom," Tuesday's cool voice broke into my half-asleep, half-awake head.

Sitting straight up, I grabbed her arm. "Holy shit, what time is it?"

"I just woke. I didn't realize you'd be asleep, and I thought you'd better get up."

Throwing back the covers, I slid from the bed. "You thought right. We have a lot to do tonight."

"Such as?"

"I know how to prove whether Kel did it or not."

"You're not sure now?"

"I only have his word. I don't think he killed anyone, other than my dreams at one point, but you don't ever really know someone, do you?" I asked, thinking about my conversation with Caleb.

"No, you don't. People can always surprise you," she replied, then stopped.

Her head lifted.

"What?" I asked quietly.

"Someone is here," she said. She sped off toward the front door.

I followed, but by the time I got to the door, Tuesday was holding it open, and glaring with her hand on her hip.

Levi Cassidy stood in my doorway, and he was wearing a cowboy hat.

Oh, my.

While I was containing my lady bits, another man stepped up next to Levi.

Levi turned. "Oh, I brought along Nathan. He's what you'd call the law in this situation. May we come in?"

Everyone looked at me. Oh, right. "Yes, please." I stood back to let them in the door.

Nathan was about the same height as Levi, and he did not have a cowboy hat. He looked like someone I'd see in Malibu on a surfboard—and he looked far too young to be the law of anything.

"Why did you bring him?" Tuesday hissed.

"That's a good question. I didn't know we were involving more people," I glared at Levi, he and his attractive cowboy hat notwithstanding.

Focus, Deana! I told myself. This was getting ridiculous.

"I felt it was the next step," Levi said.

"Well, let's not stand in the hallway. Come into the kitchen," I turned and headed back into the house. Everyone trooped in behind me, and the two men sat down at the table. Tuesday came and stood next to me with her arms crossed.

"What are you, the bodyguard?" Nathan asked.

"It's my job to keep her safe." Tuesday didn't give an inch.

"Why are you both here?" I asked. I could feel the tension ratcheting up.

"Nathan is in charge of seeing justice done within our territory."

"Oh, so you're the pet killer?" I asked, crossing my arms as well.

"When I need to be," Nathan said, not rising to the bait.

"What is it you think you can do here?" I asked.

"Grandpa, your ability to be strategic needs some work," Tuesday muttered.

"Well, actually," I held up a hand, "It's good that you're here, you being the law and all. I know how to prove that Kel didn't do it."

"Really?" Nathan asked.

"A drop of his blood," I said.

It was as though I dropped a stink bomb in the middle of the table. I couldn't see Tuesday's expression, but the two men showed me all I needed to know. Caleb was right—they weren't happy I knew about it.

"Why hasn't that been done? To be sure?" I

demanded. "Why am I the one who has to ask about this when he has less than three days to go?"

"Why are you asking about it?" Nathan had stilled. "How do you even know about this?"

"I'm good at my job," I said to him. Yeah, he was not on my Christmas card list, for sure.

"What does that mean?" Tuesday asked.

Another thing Caleb had been right about. Not all the vampires knew about it. Only Levi didn't look surprised. If anything, he looked pleased.

"It means there is a way, if the human agrees, that we can settle this. I'll need to call Delgado," Nathan said, getting up and walking to the hallway.

I was about to object that I didn't want that man in my house, and then decided that if he wanted to know where I lived, he probably could find it without even lifting a finger.

Nathan came back. "Call the human," he said.

"His name is Kel. Please refer to him as such," I snapped. I couldn't believe Levi had dragged this guy into my home. Or that he'd come himself, even with his attractive hat. Pretty damn nervy.

Nathan didn't reply, and now it was my turn to step into the hallway.

Like earlier, Kel answered on the first ring. "What's up?" he asked.

"Come to my house."

"Why?" His voice was wary.

"Because I think I can help you prove your innocence. You'll have to let them take a drop of blood."

"What?"

I shrugged, even though he couldn't see me. "That's how it's done, apparently. I don't like it either, but it's your best shot, Kel. Please come over."

"You really think so?"

"Yes," I said. Even though I hated saying it, hated having to go along with this vampire bullshit.

"Okay," he said. "I'll be there in fifteen."

"Okay," I said and hung up. "He'll be here shortly," I told the three vampires as I walked into the kitchen.

"I'm going to go wait for Delgado," Nathan said, walking by me.

I waited until I heard the front door close, and then hissed at Levi, "What the hell were you thinking? Like I want any of that bunch here?"

"It was the only way," he said. "We had to involve him. It can't come from me, or you. Although I hadn't thought about the blood."

"You knew about it and didn't suggest it?"

"I did know about it, but it's not used very often."

"I don't even want to know more," I said. "Not one word more. I don't care. If it helps Kel, that's my concern."

"And if it doesn't?" Levi's face was impassive.

"Then he gets to face the music," I said, trying to maintain calm.

No one spoke after that. I sat down, but Tuesday

stayed standing next to me like a sentinel. That told me that shit was about to get serious.

Nathan brought Kel in, and he was about to speak when he saw the vampires in the kitchen. "Deana?" he asked.

"Have a seat. We're waiting for one more guy," I said.

Kel sat, looking nervous.

I heard the front door open once more, and walked to the entrance. "Please come in," I said, knowing the drill now.

Alfonso Delgado came in, all smiles. "Deana Holliday! You are a surprising creature, indeed. I hadn't expected to see you so soon." He came to me and, leaning down, kissed both my cheeks.

He followed me into the kitchen.

Then Delgado nodded to Tuesday. "Levi," he said, inclining his head toward the other vampire. "Well, we're all here. Nathan tells me you have stumbled upon a solution. It is interesting indeed, since it's not a practice that is commonly known, but you are correct, Deana, that it would allow for the truth to be known."

"Why wasn't it done immediately?" I asked.

"It has to be a willing offering. I did not feel that there would be a willingness," he shrugged.

I wanted to slap him, but I smiled. "Well, there is."

"Oh? You've told him what will be required?"

I nodded.

"Very well. I shall do it. Your hand, please," he said to Kel, all business now.

Kel held up a hand that shook slightly.

Delgado opened his mouth, and I saw his fangs drop down. He brushed his mouth against Kel's wrist, and then set it down so fast I couldn't tell what happened. He closed his eyes and swallowed.

"Let Levi see as well," I said. Because you know, Delgado could lie.

Delgado's eyes snapped open. Nathan was on alert, and when Delgado gave a short, curt nod, Nathan took Kel's wrist and held it to Levi.

The kitchen was so quiet you could have heard a mouse sneeze.

After what seemed like forever, Delgado opened his eyes. He didn't look pleased.

"What did you see?" I asked.

His lips pursed. "Your friend tells the truth, Deana Holliday. He did not kill Jessamine."

Everyone looked toward Levi. Slowly, Levi nodded as well.

Kel let out a breath. He kind of looked like he might cry with relief, so I took over for him. "What next?"

"You are free to go," Delgado said to Kel. "You won't speak of this business to anyone."

"No," Kel said, his voice shaky. "What about Lavina?"

Really? He had to push it when he'd just gotten his life back?

"We will speak to her. That is not your concern. You need to go now," Delgado said.

Kel got up, and I hurried to his side, worried that he'd step in a big pile of shit. I could see his shoulders bunch, a sure sign of his rising temper. "Let me walk you out," I said, taking his arm and pulling him away.

He came with me, but I could feel the struggle. At the door, he turned, and hugged me. "I'm sorry, Dee. For everything. Thank you."

"You're welcome. Get out of here before you do something stupid. I'll call you tomorrow."

"Are you sure? But I—"

I stopped him. "I'm sure. Go. And don't make a fuss about Lavina. She was all right when we saw her. I'm sure you'll see her soon."

His face brightened, visible even in my darkened hallway. He gave me a one-armed hug, and then left. I stood at the door for a moment, wondering what was waiting for me back in the kitchen.

Might as well go find out.

Everyone but Tuesday was sitting at the table now. She gestured for me to sit down in front of her. I was glad she was here, on my side, glaring at all three of the men.

"Deana, I am glad to have settled that, but I am curious as to where you heard of this manner of discovering the truth." Delgado's words were pleasant, but his eyes were dark and flat. "And I will tell you that your efforts were more than that boy deserved."

"Probably, but that's my call as to where I put my effort," I said, trying not get shitty.

"Yes, I suppose so. But where did you hear of this?"

"Research. That's what I do. I'm an investigator."

He studied me for a few moments. "You are very good at this, then. That's good, very good." He tapped his chin. "I will hire you to find out who the killer is. I'll give you five days, since you managed this so admirably," he beamed at me like he was giving me a gift. "Then, if you do not discover the killer, you and I will discuss what happens when my terms are not met."

"No," Tuesday said.

"No," Levi said at the same time.

"What does that mean?" I asked.

"It means you have five days from now. I shall visit you here, in five days' time, and we shall see who the killer in our midst is." He rose. "Come, Nathan, we have work to do this evening. Thank you for your hospitality," he said to me. "Levi, Tuesday," he added, and drifted from the room.

Leaving quiet chaos in his wake.

CHAPTER ELEVEN

I waited, again, to hear the door close. But this time, I waited to hear the car start, and then, I went to the window to make sure they were leaving. As the car drove away, I turned back to the two vampires, who hadn't said one fucking word.

"Okay, what the hell just happened?" I asked. "I know it's not good, so don't spare me."

"You have five days to find out who did kill Jessamine, or..." Levi stopped.

"Or Delgado will claim you and turn you," Tuesday said flatly.

"What?" I yelped. "What in the actual hell? Where was that said and agreed on?"

"It doesn't matter if you didn't agree," said Tuesday.

"My mother was right. I shouldn't have gotten involved in this," I muttered, sitting down and slumping over the

table. "I don't have a clue where to go from here. Seriously," I looked up. "I don't know who had it in for your wife,
and I'm fresh out of ideas." I was so mad, I wanted to
scream. I stood up. "You know what? I'm out for a while."

"Where are you going?" Tuesday asked.

"For a ride. I'll be back."

"Let me know if you decide otherwise," Tuesday
said.

"I'll be back. I don't run from a fight," I said.

"No, I don't believe you do," Levi said. He sounded
sad.

Right now, I didn't care. All the vampires could go
straight to hell, or wherever they went. High handed
assholes. Just assuming the little humans would go
along with whatever!

I shot out of the garage on the Chief, liking the night
air on my face. I drove out of Venice and onto the PCH,
needing to just be out here with the bike, and not think
about anything.

Because I really didn't know what to do. And I didn't
want to die. In any way.

FOUR HOURS LATER, I pulled into the garage. When I
walked into the kitchen, Tuesday was there, reading on
a laptop. At least it wasn't mine.

"I'm glad you're back safely," she said as she looked

up. "I sent Levi home. He is not going to be any help with this."

"Who can?" I sat down, feeling very tired. "I've been over and over it in my head. It could be anyone who killed her. Levi said she was down on the beach. There are no cameras there, and we don't have anyone else to use the bite-the-wrist truth telling thing with."

"How did you know about that? I didn't even know," she said.

"I have a source," I said, not willing to out Caleb.

"It's a good one. I can see why Delgado's pissed at you. That's why he did what he did, you know. He's worried. You know more than you should, and he's worried how much more you might know. So he's got to control you."

"Who the hell does he think he is?"

"He's the guy who runs Los Angeles," Tuesday said.

"I like you, but I don't want to be a vampire," I said. "And I sure as hell don't want to have to answer to that guy."

"It's not for everyone, that's true. I take no offense. I wouldn't want to be beholden to him either." She gazed at me thoughtfully. "I need to tell Zachary of this. He is my coven leader, and if it comes out I withheld information, it will be my head."

I shrugged. "I'm not the one keeping secrets," I said. "Tell him the whole thing. Hey, where's Levi again?" She'd mentioned him, and I'd already forgotten what she said. My brain was pinging like a thousand pinballs were loose in my head.

"I sent him home. The nerve of him, bringing Nathan here. Nathan's one step above a thug, and everyone knows that. What did he think would happen?" She sounded disgusted.

"It did save Kel," I said.

"Yes, and put you in his place. You need to talk to your source again and see if there are any more ideas they haven't shared."

"What have you been doing?" I nodded at the laptop to change the subject.

She smiled. "We think alike. I was looking to see if there were any public cameras out near the house or the beach. It's a public beach."

"Any luck?"

She shook her head.

I got up. "I'm going to bed. I can't think straight."

"I'll be up until dawn."

"Thank you," I said.

She nodded and went back to the computer. I headed up to bed, to try and forget the tangle of thought and panic that was forming a big, fat ball in my head. But when I got into bed, I didn't fall asleep right away. If I couldn't come up with something by tomorrow night, I was going to have to call my mom. And my aunts.

Shit.

I closed my eyes and forced myself to relax. I needed the sleep.

WHEN I WOKE UP, the house lay quiet. All my vampire pains-in-the-asses were asleep, which meant I could focus on how to get myself out this mess.

All I wanted to do was pull the covers back up over my head, but instead, I threw them back and went forth into my day with a vengeance.

I took stock of my concerns in the shower. First, I'd cleared Kel. He was done. The Chief was mine, and I didn't have his death hanging on me anymore.

Second, I needed focus on what Caleb needed. I wasn't sure. He felt like a loose end, and he was the one holding the loose end. Maybe it was that loss of control that was making me crazy. Although he'd saved my ass with the Kel thing, so maybe he would have an idea. I willed him to come in today.

Even though he was getting ready to die, and I hated being part of that, I found that I liked him. He was a force for good, even if he seemed to take a slightly off the beaten path road to do it.

Third, I would ask him what he knew about a Volcanic. I hated the idea of pinning so much on one person, but I was at a dead end.

Thinking about problem number three, I laughed to myself in the shower. Madigan had given me thirty days to do what I thought was probably his dirty work. I wondered what would happen if I ended up a vampire under Alfonso Delgado's thumb. I'd pay some money to see those two arrogant asshats face off. I'd venture to say Madigan's suit might end up a bit ruffled.

Even though the thought of dealing with either of them wasn't really funny.

Fourth, if none of this panned out, I needed to call my mom. And my aunts. I dreaded bringing Mom into it. She was pretty low key, probably because Gran was most definitely not. But her last call showed me that she was leaning pretty hard into Gran territory and updating her on this mess would only make it worse. I sighed as I rinsed my hair. I didn't need that, but I needed to be realistic. If I needed help. I'd have to do it.

Finally, my fifth concern. How the hell was I going to discover who it was that killed Jessamine Cassidy? I had no idea who was pissed at her or wanted her dead. My introduction into the world of vampires was awkward, bumpy, and another pain in my ass.

What I did know was that I didn't want to be a vampire. And I sure didn't want to have to answer to Alfonso Delgado. How to fight him?

Another thing I didn't have the answer to.

How the hell had this gone from helping a friend to trying to save my own skin?

The cooling water alerted me I'd been in here for a long time, trying to sort out my tangled messes. I sighed, and finished up, turning off the water.

Today, I was going to plow through my emails, and get all my non-supernatural stuff in order, because my supernatural stuff seemed to be doing nothing but ramping up. I didn't want any of my clients to get less than good service.

Because even the threat of eternal undead life yoked to a psycho is not enough to stop good customer service.

Despite all my woes, I was laughing to myself as I drove to work. When I got to my office, though, my smile fell.

Kel was on a bike parked out in front of my door. I felt like I should know which one it was, but I didn't have time for that this morning. He smiled a greeting at me. Great. Can't he just be happy I saved his ass and move on? I sighed, put on what I hoped was a nice expression, and got out to face whatever it was he was bringing me.

When I walked toward him, he came off the bike and enveloped me a bear hug. It was like falling backward in time when we were real friends.

"Dee, I can't thank you enough," he said into my hair.

I stepped back. "You don't have to thank me, Kel. You asked for help, and I did the best I could. I gave you my word, and I don't go back on my word."

He smiled at me. "No, you don't, even though I've been an asshole to you for the past two years. I don't deserve you as a friend."

I laughed as I unlocked the door. "No, you don't, but I'm very glad you're not going to die for something you didn't do."

"Who killed her?" he asked as he walked in behind me.

I shrugged. "I don't know," I said over my shoulder as I started making coffee. "So, what brings you in today?"

"I wanted to apologize. I made things more difficult than they had to be when Derek died."

Facing him, I gave him my 'no bullshit' look. "Yes, you did. And it hurt."

He looked down. "I know. I have no excuse. I was so —I missed him so much."

"Yeah, so did I," I leaned against the counter.

"I know. And I shit all over that. I can't make that up to you, and for that, I'm sorry. When you agreed to take this case, I thought, Wow. She didn't have to. I've been doing a lot of thinking this week."

"Impending death has that effect," I said.

"Yes, it does. And I know I can't make this right, that we'll never be friends like we were." There was genuine regret in his voice.

My voice softened. "No, we can't." I wasn't going to sugar coat it.

"But for me, this falls under unfinished business. I'm saying thank you again, and giving you these," he stood up and put a set of keys on my desk.

"What are they to?"

He jerked his head toward the parking lot. "Didn't you recognize it? It was Derek's. The Sin Bin."

The Sin Bin was what Derek had called the bike he was restoring for himself. The last time I'd seen it, it had still been in pieces. In addition to the band, Derek and Kel had loved their bikes. Derek hadn't been a spendthrift except with his bike addiction. The Sin Bin was a 1942 Harley Davidson UL74 Flathead, and he'd found it in a pile in some guy's backyard in Pennsylvania. The entire time we were together, he had worked on it. The sidecar wasn't original—he'd decided to add it when he found that in another pile in some moldering backyard a year or so later. It wasn't a Harley Davidson—it was... I couldn't remember what it was. But it was a bike just for Derek, and in the years since he'd died, I'd forgotten about it.

"Did you finish it?" I walked to the door to see the gleaming black bike. She was gorgeous.

"I felt like I had to. He loved it so much," Kel came to stand behind me.

"You don't have to do this," I eased away from him. I didn't want to fall back into the comfortable relationship we'd had. Those times were over.

"I do. You saved my life, and you, more than anyone else in my life, had the right to tell me to fuck off and best of luck. And you didn't. Let me do this. It eases my conscience."

I looked at him. He seemed sincere. "All right. Thank you. Now where's the title?"

Kel burst into laughter. "I love that about you, Dee! You don't waste time with bullshit."

I smiled. "No, I don't. There are better things to be doing."

Kel pulled papers out of his pocket and set them on the desk with the keys. "There it is. It's yours. Honestly, it belongs with the Chief."

Unexpectedly, I found tears welling in my eyes. Derek had said that. I felt like I'd finally been able to move forward from that part of my life—and this week was bringing it all up again.

Although maybe not in a bad way.

"So, I'm out of here. Thank you. If you need anything, you call me. I know I blew it, but I owe you forever," Kel said. He stepped closer to me, kissed me on the cheek, and left.

I stood watching him, lost in thought.

Then I went out to see the Flathead. Running my hand across the gas tank, I saw the words 'Sin Bin' painted on it. It wasn't Derek's handwriting. Kel must have done it.

Combined with all the things going on this week, I suppose it was natural that I stood there, petting a motorcycle, and crying.

CHAPTER TWELVE

BRUSHING MY EYES, I WENT BACK INTO MY OFFICE. IT looked like another trip to Motor Vehicles was in order. I didn't know how to feel, and honestly, at this point, I didn't have the time to sit and mull this over. Which kind of pissed me off.

This whole week had been me reacting to the shit going on around me. It was time for me to take back the control of my life. If I was going down, it was going to be on my terms. Not the terms of some vampire who bought his own hype.

I locked the door, pulled the blinds, and put the Closed sign back on. Then I sat down and called Deadwood.

Deirdre answered. "Hello, Deana. I'm glad you called. Your mom is going bananas, even though she's trying not to show it."

"Well, this call isn't going to make her feel better. But I'll be coming clean," I said.

"Oh, shit. Should I put this on speaker?"

"Probably a good idea."

"All right, hang on. I'm going to yell." It sounded like she put the phone against her leg, but I could still hear her yelling to the house.

They weren't quiet at the house on Pearl Street. The thought made me smile.

"Okay, I have everyone here. I'm putting you on speaker. What's going on, Deana?"

I sighed, bracing myself for the onslaught. "I'm up a creek with a vampire."

There was silence on the other end, and then Desdemona said, "How the hell did you end up the creek? Wasn't this just you going and talking to Zachary?"

This was going to be more difficult than I thought. "It's all complicated and basically, a shit show. Let me tell you, and then you can yell at me later, okay?"

"She's totally one of us," one of the aunts muttered. I couldn't tell which one said it, but there was a ripple of laughter on their end.

Painstakingly, I went through the whole thing. When I stopped, they were all silent.

"Well," Deirdre said. "You are up a creek."

"Good to know your assessment of the situation is accurate," Daniella said.

"Mom?" I asked.

"I'm trying to calm myself, Deana," my mom said quietly.

"Couldn't you have said no?" Gran asked. "Kel was such a... such a shit!"

"Gran, that's quite the condemnation," I said. She didn't normally swear. "He was, but I have to say, he's redeemed himself. We're not besties, or anything, but things are okay now, and he did that."

"Well, so did you, by saving his behind," Gran snapped.

A wave of longing swept over me that made me want to lay down. I wasn't used to being on my own, as much as I'd thought it would be a good thing. I missed them, and I found that I missed this sense of extended family that going to see my aunts had brought to us.

"Let's break this down. The demon, Madigan? I'm not familiar with him, but it's not a good thing that he knows about Ashlar," Desdemona took charge as she usually did. "There's a reason he thinks you know where to find that pistol, Deana."

"I had the same thought, but I don't have a clue why."

"You still have time. Wait and see, and just be observant. He knows something he's not telling. Shifty bastards," she added.

"That was kind of my plan, but it's good to hear that you'd do the same."

"What else can you do?" Daniella asked.

"Tell them all to go away and leave her alone!" Gran chimed in.

"Gran, it doesn't work that way," I said. "What I would like is some vampire spray. You know, like you spray ants? So I can make Delgado go away."

"He's such an ass," Deirdre said.

"It's amazing how you all never leave, and you know everything, and everyone knows you," I said. "I've been name dropping, I have to admit."

"Deana, we're coming home," Mom said.

"No, Mom! No! I don't want you pulled into this. They know where I live, they probably know more than I'd ever want them to. If you're here, you're a weapon against me."

More silence.

"She's right," Gran said. "I hate to admit it, because I want to tell you to come here and we'll all kick their asses—"

"Gran!" I said. "The aunts are rubbing off on you!"

Everyone laughed, which was a much better thing than silence.

"Well, we will. And they can all leave you alone."

"DeAnna, now that you're out—well, Deana is—she needs to stand up and be strong," Daniella said to Gran. "Part of why no one gives us a lot of grief anymore is that we've never backed down. Deana is one of us. She needs to not back down. Which, by the way, it sounds like you've been doing great at," she said to me.

"I'm trying. They're scary."

"They used to be human, but now they are more, and less," Desdemona said. "You have to remember that when dealing with them."

"How can you forget?" I asked. "But Tuesday—the vampire Zachary sent to help me—I really like her. She seems sincere."

"She's protected you," Deirdre said. "That counts for something in their world."

"Who is this Caleb Black?" Mom asked. "You mention him, and he saved your bacon with helping Kel, but who is he?"

I shook my head. "It's weird. He says he's like a wendigo, but he doesn't eat people. He eats bad spirits, and he was created by a shaman in his tribe."

"Are you sure he's a good guy?" Mom asked.

"I think so," I said.

"Why?" Gran asked.

"Because my gut says so. I like him. He likes all of you."

"That's good enough for me," Desdemona said. "My biggest screw ups have been when I didn't trust my gut instincts. So. Let's focus on the immediate problem. Vampire spray," she said with a laugh. "I could sell a metric ton if we actually manage to make it. On the very down low, of course."

"I'm really glad I called you all," I said.

"Why didn't you do it earlier?" Mom asked.

"Because I didn't want to worry you," I said honestly.

"I've been worried," she said simply. "I can tell when you're in trouble."

I sighed. "I know, Mom. I'm sorry."

"If there's one thing the last month has taught us, we're stronger together," Mom said.

"Isn't that what I've been saying?" Gran exclaimed. I'd bet she'd thrown her hands up, too.

"I have some ideas," Deirdre said, getting to the business at hand. "If your ears are burning for the next couple of days, Deana, just know that your mom is complaining. But we'll let her vent at us."

"Thanks," Mom said dryly.

"How about two days? I have just under five days to figure this mess out," I said.

"All right. You call us, Deana. If we don't hear from you in forty-eight hours, we're sending in the calvary," Desdemona said.

"Dee, please be careful," Mom said.

"I'm trying as hard as I can, Mom," I said.

"That's what worries me, honey," she replied.

"Come on, lazy—oh, hey, Doc," Desdemona said.

"Darlin'?" I heard my many times great grandfather on the phone. Which was weird as hell because he was a ghost.

"Hey, Doc," I said.

"Are you all right?" he asked.

"Not really. But I think I will be."

"You mean you finally took your head out of your backside and leaned on your family?"

"Wow. Shamed by the family ghost," I said.

"That's what we're here for, darlin'," he said, and I could hear the lurking humor in his words. "To tell all you still locked in the mortal coil what you're doin' wrong."

"You're so good at it, too," Desdemona said. "Deana, keep the faith. This happens to us all the time. The way forward will show itself."

"I hate to say it, but listen to Miss Wise Guru," Deirdre added.

"Okay. I'm going to hang up now," I said. "Love you," I added.

"Love you," they all chorused together at me. Desdemona told me, when I was in Deadwood, that her mother, Meema, had always told them before they went into the fray, to make sure to let those you loved know it. Subsequently, it was how they ended all conversations.

I loved that family tradition. As I set the phone back on my desk, I felt better than I had since Kel walked into my office. Remembering my mental list that I'd made in the shower, I got into my email, and caught up with all my clients who were not dying on me, threatening to kill me, or wanting to turn me into something else.

I spent the rest of the day taking care of all the things that had been piling up. I hated that it felt like I was settling my affairs, but after this was over, and I made it through, I wanted to have a business to come back to. No one else came to see me—not my sort-of wendigo, or a demon, or anyone.

Hearing back on my digging with the local cops, I was able to email Zachary, thank him again for sending Tuesday to me, and give him the information he sought. Doing so crossed off another item on my list.

Which was a nice change. I mapped out a plan of action that I could take that might keep me from being a Delgado groupie—if I could just find a way to get away from him. That was the key. Whether it would work was another thing entirely, but I had a plan. And that was something.

At six, I closed up the office and went home to wait for my vampires—friends and foes—to wake up.

CHAPTER THIRTEEN

I WAS OUT ON THE DECK OVERLOOKING THE CANAL WHEN Tuesday walked out. "How are you?" she asked.

"Better than I probably ought to be. We need to get Levi over here. And," I stood up, "I want to thank you."

"For what?"

"You're still here, helping me. You were supposed to help me with the Kel matter. That's solved. But you're still here."

Tuesday was slow in answering. "This is technically still the Kel matter. While you have cleared him, you have been given a responsibility that is not really yours to bear."

"Well, there's that," I said.

"Delgado is getting too big for himself," she muttered.

"When wasn't he?" I asked. "Seriously, that guy has balls to spare."

"Zachary chooses not to make waves, but no one is really fond of Delgado."

"Well, I can't see why. He's such a peach," I said.

"Fear. He's ruthless. So is Levi, by the way."

"Whoa. That was kind of a left turn," I said.

"I know you find him... attractive."

"Double whoa. Why would you think that?"

Tuesday smiled, coming sit at the table with me. "Your heart beats faster, and your face gets flushed."

"Shit," I said.

She laughed.

I stared. "This isn't funny."

"It's very funny. He's not a bad vampire, not like Delgado. And I have no objection to humans and vampires being together. I am just warning you. He and Jessamine were able to stay away from being brought into any covens, or clans, and there's a reason."

"Well, isn't that the way of any vampire who makes it to, say, fifty?"

"What do you mean?" She turned her intense gaze to me.

"If you manage to stay alive as a vampire, you're strong. Don't you have to be?" I shrugged. It made sense to me.

"Yes. This is not a life for the weak."

"Kind of what I thought. So, we need to see Levi, and see who had a beef with him, or Jessamine, or both."

"There's more to this than just finding a killer," Tuesday said.

"What do you mean?"

She stood up. "I mean I need to go out. I know it isn't your way, but can I ask you to stay here?"

"Wait, you can't leave me hanging like this!" I stood up, making to follow her.

She held out a hand. "No, I need to go poking around on my own. I don't want to expose you any further. Please, Deana? I'll call Levi," amazingly her voice took on a teasing tone, "And send him over so you can look at him and ask him all sorts of questions."

"Tuesday, just because I find him appealing doesn't mean a thing. It means I like to look at him. But that's all it means."

"Well, if it keeps you here, that's fine with me. Please, stay here."

"Oh, all right."

"Good. I'll call him before I go." She slipped from the deck.

I watched her disappear, and then sat down again.

An hour later, I heard the doorbell. When I went to answer it, I looked through the door viewer. It was Levi, complete with cowboy hat.

Why did he have to look so good?

Opening the door, I said, "I see you've been called in to babysit."

Levi stepped in, removing his hat. "I wouldn't call it babysitting. Tuesday wants to be sure you're safe."

"Or that I don't run away," I said as I walked back into the kitchen.

"You don't seem the type to run," Levi commented.

"I'm not. I'm also not in the mood for company. Would you mind if I went to bed?"

"Of course not," Levi said.

"You're welcome to make yourself at home," I said. "I'm upstairs if things go sideways," I added.

I headed for the steps when I heard him say, "Goodnight, Deana."

"Goodnight," I said.

Even though part of me wanted to stay down there, I went to my room and closed my door. I'd stay up here and go to sleep if it killed me. And tomorrow, I'd manage this on my own.

WITH MY CURRENT situations of vampires every night, it was a relief to get up and have a silent house. I checked my phone—nothing from Deadwood. Which was fine. I got up and was at the office an hour before I opened. I'd remembered that Caleb had given me a card. It was time to stop pretending I knew how to navigate this world and ask for help.

Which would have been a great plan, but I couldn't find the card.

I was going to end up a vampire, and then I was going to end up dead, because I'd kill that ass Delgado.

Or at least I'd try. If I could just find a way to get away from his damn deadline! Getting away after that would be cake. Comparatively, anyway.

"Damn it," I said, pacing my back hallway.

The bell rang, and as if called, Caleb walked in.

"Oh, my god, am I glad to see you!" I exclaimed.

"You are? You were so angry when I saw you before," he said. He shifted his brown bag under his arm.

It took me a moment to remember what had happened—oh, yeah. The whole 'there's a demon branch in the family tree' thing. "That doesn't matter now," I said. "You were right about the blood memory. My friend is completely in the clear. And—"

"I have to talk to you, Deana," Caleb said, sitting down heavily. "My time is close. I need to give you some things, and tell you about what I'm leaving you."

Shit. Shit. Shit. "Now? You're sure?" I asked. My issues seemed a lot less important.

"I am. I can feel the end coming. First, I give you all of my possessions." He pulled a folder out of his jacket and laid it on the desk. "It's all in there, and it's straight-forward. It's all legal. I'm turning everything over to you. Contact the attorney, his information is in there as well." He pushed the folder to me.

"This isn't exactly ethical," I said. I was pretty sure there were a lot of laws against this. Great. If I lived, I'd be sued by the state. That is, if I lived. Because not all my plan was in place.

"It's legal," he repeated. "I made sure of it. As far as

the attorney knows, I'm going to India on a spiritual journey." He smiled, and I could see that these measures, this putting things in order, had given him a sense of peace.

"But that's not the important thing. This is," he took the bag from under his arm and laid it on the desk reverently.

"What is this?" I asked.

Without saying anything, he reached in and pulled out the item in it.

My life went from really messed up to completely screwed.

"Holy shit," I said.

CHAPTER FOURTEEN

I KNEW THIS WAS IT. I JUST KNEW IT. THE QUESTION WAS, how did Madigan know?

"Do you know a demon named Madigan?" I asked.

Caleb's head jerked at the name. "He's been here?"

"Looking for a Volcanic pistol. Is this what he's looking for?" I gestured at the pistol on my desk, not wanting to touch it.

My gut was screaming out that the red flags were at hurricane status.

"Yes," Caleb said.

"And you're giving it to me?"

"You must be the guardian of it now."

"No!" I stood up, backing away from the desk. "This past week, all I've done is what everyone else has told me I have to. I don't have to take this! I don't! I won't!"

"You must," Caleb said. "You must take it, and hide

it, and you must promise me that you will hide it until you find a way to destroy it."

"What's the big deal with this thing?"

"Many years ago, I helped a demon. In return, she gave this to me. She thought she was doing me a favor. She knew it couldn't fall into the hands of humans, and there were no other supernaturals she felt would bear the responsibility appropriately. She didn't even trust herself," he said, a sad smile crossing his face.

"What does it do?"

"This can kill any living thing. No matter how magical, no matter how powerful—one shot from this, and it will die."

"Jesus," I sat back down.

"So, now you see. There's no way I can give this to anyone else. But you are trustworthy, and honorable— you can handle this, Deana."

"Caleb, I don't want this. This is too much for anyone to handle."

"I know this," he said. "I considered burying it with me, but I'm worried who might dig it up. There are rumors I've got it. No one knows anything, but the rumors persist."

"What am I supposed to do with it?" I asked, feeling panic rising within me.

"Hide it. Keep it safe."

"If people—like Madigan—know you're got it, and he must have known you came to see me, won't he come after me?"

"Yes," Caleb said. "But you can fool him. You've got the strength to do this, Deana. I knew it when I met you."

I sighed, shaking my head, and looking away. I didn't want to see the expression on his face. "I can't do this, Caleb. There are other things that might make me a bad choice." I was thinking about the fact that I could be a vampire in a couple of days. What would I do with this then?

"You must promise me, swear a pact with me on your honor, the honor of the Nightingales, that you will keep this safe. If Madigan, or anyone else like him got it —" he closed his eyes, and a shudder ran through him —"The world would no longer be safe for anyone. Not humans, not supernaturals—no one."

He had a point. Damn him.

The silence was getting awkward as I thought over everything he'd said. A sane person would walk away from this. But I wasn't sane. I was a Holliday and a Nightingale, and we faced things head on. For the most part, anyway. Even with my looming life change, I couldn't say no to him.

"All right," I said finally. "I'll do it."

Caleb rose. "Then you must make a pact with me," he said formally. He stood up, indicating that I needed to do the same. "Give me your hand, *câpân*."

I held it out, and he came around to my side of the desk, taking it in his own. I had the same sense I'd had before when I touched his hand—of a large person, of safety, of protection. Having that feeling made me see how often I didn't feel safe.

Still holding my hand in his, he whipped out a small knife, and before I could protest, cut first his hand, and then mine. He held them together and something—not just blood—passed between us. I stared at him.

"Swear to me, Deana Holliday, that you will take this trust, and you will keep this safe," Caleb said, his voice low.

"I swear I will keep it safe."

"For the rest of your life."

"For the rest of my life."

"And you will pass this on to another such as yourself."

"And I will pass this on to another such as myself." God help them, I thought.

He gripped my hand tighter, and it was as though I'd stuck my finger in a light socket. There was an actual shock that passed through me. I staggered, and blinked.

Caleb licked his finger, and then passed it over the cut he'd made in my hand. It healed as though he'd never cut me.

"Whoa," I said.

"You have sworn your pact with me, and I entrust you with this," Caleb said formally. "I thank you, Deana Holliday. You have allowed me to go to the spirit land of my father with peace."

"I'm glad," I said, and I meant it, even with the weight of what I'd agreed to weighing heavily on me.

"I must go now, *câpân*. It's my time. Hide it, and then go through the papers I have left you. They will show you your path." He patted my hand.

It was hard to wrap my head around all of this. "What do I do now?"

"Hide it. Then read the papers." Caleb moved to the door. "I will see you again," he said.

Then he was gone.

I stared at the pistol on my desk. Son of a bitch. I had to hide it. I snatched it up, and ran to the back office. I put it in the safe and closed the door gratefully, glad to have it out of my sight.

There was no way I could ever use this or let anyone know I had it. The target on my back would be larger than life. I couldn't tell my family. I couldn't tell anyone. Anyone I told would be a potential target, and if I judged incorrectly, they'd try to take it from me.

It was a metric shit ton of power.

All locked in my safe. I'd have to come up with a better way to hide it. Something like Caleb's crumpled brown bag.

Oh, shit. I ran back out to the front office and found the bag still on the desk. Anyone looking for him, say a demon named Madigan, could walk in here and see the bag—I had to get rid of it.

Feeling paranoid as hell, I burned it over my trash can. Then I sat down and opened the file. Time to see if anything in here could save me. Because otherwise, I'd have to find a Volcanic exit plan, and hide this thing.

I looked at the first page. It was a will and attached at the top with a paper clip was a business card for an attorney. Okay. All fine and normal. I set that aside and looked at the next page. It was a deed to a house in— where the hell was Bisbee?

When I looked online, it was a tiny town in Arizona. What the hell would I be doing in Arizona? Nothing, if I could help it. It was so hot there.

The next page was a list of bank accounts—"Holy hell," I said. Whatever Caleb had been doing, it had paid well. He had a hefty sum in his name. Now in my name. When he'd said he didn't have a lot, he'd been seriously underestimating things.

I was so getting audited. I could feel it. Getting inheritances from clients? The state would be salivating over such a juicy target. But I'd need to deal with that later. Hopefully, he'd told the attorney something good about why I was his heir.

The next page was the best. The absolute best. I remembered Caleb telling me that he chatted with people in online forums. He'd left me a list of all his logins. Which made me laugh. He was so old-fashioned, so formal. And here were all his logins, like anyone else in this day and age.

Clicking on to the forums, I started to read. I couldn't believe how open people were. Didn't they know this was the internet, and nothing ever went away? That nothing was private? I glanced at Caleb's notes again, and he'd written, *I don't often comment, but I try to read to stay aware of what's going on. You might be able to find out more about the vampire's death.*

That would be nice. Really fucking nice, as a matter of fact. I went to the forums specifically for vampires. There was a thread dedicated to Who Killed Jessamine? Some of the comments were completely out of control —it was kind of funny to see that vampires had the same conspiracy theory nutters that the rest of the world did.

No one knew why she'd been targeted. Outside of her recent argument with Lavina, which everyone seemed to know about, and which some people were sure Lavina had organized it because that was up her alley, no one disliked Jessamine. At least, not that they were admitting.

They were afraid of Levi. That came through. I remembered Tuesday telling me that Levi was strong, and he'd protected himself and Jessamine for years from being dragged into a clan, or politics, or whatever it was vampires did.

On a whim, I searched out my aunts' name. There were a number of threads about them, and there was one about the recent kerfuffle in Deadwood. How did people hear about it? There had been no one there outside of the family—and then I saw that Deirdre had actually made a post asking if anyone knew about a witch. She called her a hedge witch. That term made no sense to me, so I wrote it down to look up later. No one had mentioned this to me, but that was interesting.

This would explain how so many people knew my aunts. I stopped myself. I could go down that rabbit hole all day, and I was on the clock. As interesting as this all was, I was no closer to finding out who had killed Jessamine.

So she didn't have any enemies—not any that were publicly declaring themselves. No one felt she needed to die, or was a pain in their ass, to their agenda, or anything else they were willing to state openly.

That meant someone had killed her for a reason that was hidden, and that didn't spell good news for anyone. Since no one was talking, I'd need to go to Levi. I needed him to go through her journal, see if there was anything concerning.

And they were married—I assumed that was what being mated meant. Wouldn't she have told him if there was someone who had a beef with her? That would be normal, standard.

Which put me back into waiting for nightfall to find Levi and question him. I sighed. This 'only available at night' was such a pain in the ass.

I spent the next two hours reading through the forum, fascinated. There was so much more to this world than I thought. In addition to vampires, there were shifters of all varieties, including dragons. Fairies, fae—I wasn't sure of the difference, although it seemed to be wing based—goblins, trolls, dwarves, yeti, witches, wizards, necromancers—I knew about them—and pretty much anything I'd ever read or seen a movie about. Not all the supernaturals were online, but there were discussion boards for all of them.

This was all great, but it hadn't helped me find a killer. Well, it told me that there was a killer, and he or she did this wanting to hide it. Because goodwill for Jessamine was falling from the sky, according to these boards.

I looked at the clock. It wasn't quite closing time, but I figured it had been quiet after the first hour, so I could cut out and go home early. I found that I was tired, and wanted to nap before Tuesday got up, and I asked her to ferret out where Levi might be. I mean, I *knew* where he was, but he hadn't given me permission to call, or come by again, and I worried that he might not want to help me.

Then again, maybe he would. It was in his best interest to discover if someone was harboring a secret grudge toward his wife.

The house was quiet when I came in, and I went straight up to my room after leaving a note for Tuesday on the kitchen island. I fell asleep faster than I'd thought, considering my head was full of everything I'd read today.

The rollercoaster was rattling up the hill, and the rattle increased until it was shaking my entire body. I opened my eyes to see Tuesday looming over me.

"Ahh!" I half-yelled.

"I came up to wake you as you asked," she said. "What's on the agenda this evening?"

"Where'd you go last night?"

"To tell Zachary all that has gone on. He is secretly pleased that you have saved your friend. He believes, as I do, that this was part of some plot on the part of Delgado, and he's happy to see it thwarted."

"Does he have any idea who might have killed her?"

Tuesday sat down, shaking her head. "No. And I believe him when he says he doesn't."

"Okay, well I had an idea. I spent some time on the message boards—"

"How did you find out about those?"

"Witches are on the boards," I shot back. "It's not like I'm not part of the people who hang there."

Her lips pursed. "That's true. Then it's good you were able to access them." Her lips pursed slightly, and I could tell she wanted to know badly how I'd managed it, but I wasn't breathing a word about my source. Like my aunts wouldn't have told me? I didn't understand why this, of all things, was a big deal.

"Anyway, everyone was saying how wonderful she was, what a loss to the community this was, who could have wanted her dead, and it came to me that this was carefully planned. Someone knew she and Lavina fought. Someone wanted this to look like a fight that got out of hand. Someone had it in for her, and wanted it secret."

"Well, of course."

"You're not getting it," I said, sitting up. "You said last night that there was more to it. I'm agreeing, and saying it's probably worse than we think. We need to call Levi, and have him go through the journal to see what else she might have seen, who might have been upset with her."

"That's a good idea."

"Do you think he'll do it?" I asked.

"Why wouldn't he? He wants to find the killer as much as you do."

"Can you call him?"

She gave me a look, and then pulled her cell from her pocket, and made the call. "Do you want him to come here?"

I nodded.

"Yes," she said. She hung up. "He's on his way."

"Then I'd better get my ass up," I sighed. "I'm just so tired."

"This is a challenging week. I find that I'm ready to rest at the dawning as well," she said.

Were we exchanging confidences? It felt like it. I smiled, and Tuesday drifted out of the room. I didn't envy the vampires for much, but every single one I'd met, even the thuggish ones, moved with a grace that was gorgeous.

Fifteen minutes later, I'd restored myself, called my mom to update her, since I didn't need her and the aunts sending in any sort of calvary. She let me know they were close to something that could help me, which cheered me.

I was in the kitchen having a cup of coffee when the doorbell rang. Tuesday went to answer it, and returned with Levi. He was carrying the small leather journal.

"How can I help you?" His deep voice and western accent rolled through the room.

I could listen to him talk forever. He could read my water bill with that voice. "Can you look through the journal and see if she had any problems, or trouble-some readings—"

"Scrying," he interjected.

"Okay, if she had any troublesome interactions with anyone else. Because whoever did this wants us to think it was Lavina. I think they knew that Delgado and the vamp cops would think it was her putting Kel up to it."

"Why would you say that?"

"Did Delgado look all that surprised when the blood memory showed that it wasn't Kel?" I'd been going over that moment in my head, and something about it had been bothering me, but until this moment, it hadn't all come together.

"He looked irritated," Tuesday snickered.

"Well, yes, but he didn't look surprised," I said again.

"No, he did not," Levi said slowly.

"And he knew the blood memory could have cleared Kel and Lavina. But he didn't do it. Why?"

"That's a good question," Levi said, meeting my eyes.

"I think the answer is in that journal," I said. "If you translate, we'll write it out, and then we can compare it to the message boards, and anyone else you think we might need to look at."

Levi nodded. "That's not a bad plan."

"It's not great, but it's the best I have," I said.

"Let's get started. We're down to four days until Delgado comes looking for answers," Tuesday said.

CHAPTER FIFTEEN

Two days later, after working two nights in a row, we hadn't found anything that Levi felt was worth pursuing. And he'd been good about following up on anything that looked promising. Watching him questioning people, even over the phone, showed me why Tuesday had warned me about him.

He was ruthless. But even that ruthlessness didn't yield a solid lead.

"I need to go to bed," I said. "I'm so tired, and I have to go to work tomorrow."

"Go ahead," said Tuesday from her station at her laptop. "I'll get you up if we find anything."

"Thanks," I said.

"Sleep well," Levi said, his eyes following me as I went upstairs.

That was the last thing I saw before I fell asleep. When I woke, the sun was shining in my window. They hadn't found anything, then. I was down to just over twenty-four hours. For the first time, I felt a wave of despair.

We weren't going to find anything. My phone ringing on the bedside table dragged me from serious moping.

It was my mom. "Hey," I said.

"We've sent the vamp spray," she said.

"Call it by its rightful name!" I heard someone yell in the background.

Mom sighed. "All right, all right. Keep your hair on. The Vamp NoMo spray should be there today."

I burst out laughing. "Who named that? Gran?" I said, overcome with giggling at the thought. Gran was the most proper of the three of us, but Deadwood had a weird effect. She could have. "You actually made it!"

"We did, And no, Gran did not name it," Mom said. "As I'm sure you know. It was Daniella. We shipped it express, and it should be there shortly, according to the tracking number."

"What does it do?"

"Spray it at the vampire in question, and they'll fall down in a deep sleep, giving you about seven and a half minutes to get away."

"What, you tested it?"

"Sort of," Mom hedged.

"What does that mean? This is my ass, Mom."

"Well, there's a zombie in the basement at the shop," she said quickly.

"What? Why do you—you know what? Never mind. I don't want to know right now. But I will be asking for details later. So when you sprayed the zombie, it knocked them for seven plus minutes?"

"Yes. On average. Sometimes, it went a little longer. But I think if you plan for six minutes, you'll be fine."

"I love you, Mom," I said, grinning. "I have until tomorrow. So if things go to shit, I'm out of here. I'll lock up the house."

"Just send me a text. Tell me that you burned a pan, or something," she said.

"Mom, thanks. I know you have other things to do."

"Well, none of us are on a deadline, so this was more important. How are things on your end?"

"Not as good as yours. The Vamp NoMo spray is timely," I said.

"Dee, if it comes to that, you run your ass off. You get far away, and don't even text me. But I would appreciate it if you locked down everything whenever you leave the house."

"I'm doing it now. I need to go into the office, Mom, so I'm going to go."

"I wish I was there," she said.

"I'm glad you're not. It would make me worry more. No one's going to come at you up there."

"That's not necessarily a comfort."

"Nothing is right now. Except NoMo spray."

We both laughed, and then said, "Love you," at the same time.

When I got up, I felt hopeful. I had an exit strategy. I'd just need to manage to hide the spray on my person and then use it if needed. Sounded simple, but it would take some planning on my part.

I decided to go into the office late, to wait on the spray. I wanted to be able to carry it with me at all times now, now that I was down to less than two full days.

The package came within two hours, and I tossed it in my bag, and took Baby and headed out. I didn't feel safe on either of the bikes at the moment. When I got to the office, I glanced around the parking lot. This had been the week for people waiting on me, so if there was someone there today, I wanted a heads up.

But the lot was clear. I hurried into the office to check out the spray. As expected, there were tons of notes about how to use it. Desdemona had written, *It works on humans too. We sprayed each other and your mom. Gives you about three minutes.*

Then in Gran's writing, *Three minutes is a good middle ground. I should know, as I sprayed all of them and timed it.*

Reading their words, smelling the herbal scents that had hitched a ride along with the package, I laughed. And felt better. A lot better. There were five small spray bottles, like travel spray. Thin, easily hidden in a pocket.

One long pump and then two for good measure, was written in a small tag tied to the top. Easily removed, and allowed me to keep the purpose secret.

I went and looked out in the parking lot again. For lunchtime, it was pretty dead. So I locked the door, pulled the blinds, and went into my back office and locked that door for good measure. Then I sat on the futon, pulled out my phone, started a timer and sprayed myself three times in the face.

When I opened my eyes again, I scrabbled for my phone. Three minutes, and fifty seven seconds. So three minute was a good time frame. And I didn't remember a thing after I sprayed myself in the face. At least I smelled good. I washed my face and hands off, and tucked the spray into my front pocket. It looked like body spray. And since I was supposedly a witch, I could claim it was something I made. You know, if I was searched at all at some point. Lavender and vanilla were the top notes, so it disguised whatever was in this well.

I made a promise right then and there to go spend more time in Deadwood, to learn what I needed to learn. But right now, I had to plan my escape. This would help me get away from Delgado and whatever goons he brought, if I was fast. I left the Closed sign on the door, although I checked my email. I'd sent out a couple of invoices, and what do you know? The bank account told me that they'd been paid.

Amazing. Perhaps things were looking up.

Zachary had gotten back to me, to let me know that he had in fact spoken with Tuesday, wished me luck in my endeavors, and appreciated the information I'd gotten for him.

With the spray helping my exit strategy, I got to work on the rest of it. Making a few phone calls after scanning the local For Sale ads got me what I needed. I needed to be ready to go. Like, walk out the door and go. I stopped, thinking. Should I tell Tuesday? She'd been an ally. I liked Levi—well my girly bits liked Levi—but I didn't feel sure about him like I felt, for the most part, about Tuesday.

Oh, shit. If I left, I needed to take the damn pistol. I couldn't leave that here. So when I left that afternoon to pick up the things I'd bought, I took it with me, feeling like I was carrying a rattlesnake in my pocket. It made me jumpy as hell—like I was putting out a beacon or something to all the non-humans in the area.

But I reminded myself that Caleb had carried this for who knew how long in a paper bag. So maybe there was no beacon.

I picked up both the items I bought, and went back to the house. It was still daylight, so that gave me the chance to get things sorted in my garage. No matter where I went, Baby, the Chief, and the Sin Bin were coming with me.

Which could be a weak spot, but there were some things a girl couldn't compromise on.

Next was my room. I started packing. As I was adding yet more tee shirts to the bag, I stopped. This was my whole life. My entire life. And I was going to toss it into a couple of bags and boxes, and leave it.

Goddamn that Alfonso Delgado. I was going to get out of this, and I was going to make him pay for doing this shit to me. Arrogant asshat. Get out of this, and then plot revenge.

"Good plan, Deana," I said. Then I zipped up my bags and brought them to the car. As I was getting the back of Baby loaded up, my cell rang.

"Hello?"

"Deana?" It was Caleb, and he sounded weak.

"Oh my god, Caleb, what's going on?"

"It's time. But I need you to come and see me."

"Where are you?" As much crap as he'd tossed onto me, he'd also made it possible for me to leave, and be comfortable. I couldn't forget that. He hadn't just tossed me to the wolves, dragons, vampires, and all the other things that would want what I had.

"I'm at the Santa Monica pier. Under it, in fact. On the southern side. Please come, Deana," he said.

"On my way," I said. Sliding into the front seat, I sped out of the house and up the highway. He sounded bad. I'm glad he'd reconsidered on the whole going off to die like a cat, hidden and alone.

Once I got to the pier, I got Baby parked and ran down along the south side of the pier. I'd heard the water in the background, and the pier opened up so that you could walk under it once you hit the water. Thankfully, there still sunlight, and I hurried through the maze of pilings, looking for him.

He was sitting against a piling with his feet in the water. I kneeled down, and couldn't contain my gasp. He was pale, and looked like every bit of the two hundred years old he was. In his lap lay a drum, and a small leather wrapped mallet was in his other hand.

Caleb looked over when he realized I was there. "That was... fast."

"Sounded like I needed to be."

A smile appeared briefly. "Yes, I think you do. Will you play for me?" His hand nudged the drum.

"Caleb, I don't—"

"It should be played by someone who cares," he said. "I think you care."

"I do." Tears welled in my eyes. I eased the drum from his hand, and fumbled a bit, getting a hold on it. It was a round hand drum with a loop at the top. I slid my fingers through the loop and then took the mallet.

"Just play. Softly." Caleb's eyes were closed. "I need a rhythm."

I hit the drum with the mallet a few times.

"Faster," Caleb said.

Picking up the tempo, I nearly dropped the drum when he began to sing. His eyes were closed, and in the darkened area under the pier, I could see that he had tears tracking down his face.

California being what it is, no one even batted an eye that the two of us were here making the song of a dying man. I kept an eye out, because the last thing Caleb needed was someone taking a picture or video of this moment.

His head turned to me and he opened his eyes as he sang. His voice got softer, and then it drifted. His hand lifted and stilled my hand that held the mallet. "Thank you," he said. "I could have... done this myself, but I found I wanted to see you once more, *câpân.*"

"What does that mean?" I asked. He'd called me that before.

"You can... look it up... later. It just means I think highly of you. That is all." His eyes held mine, and then he looked out at the water. "She's... here."

"What?" I whipped around.

Sure enough. I could see the head, and then the body of a woman in the waves. "Who is she?" I whispered.

"Yareli, the water lady," Caleb said.

I glanced at him. He was smiling. It was a genuine smile, one of love. I looked at the woman again. She wasn't coming any closer.

Caleb put his arm on mine and I realized that he was trying to stand. "Hey, what are you doing?"

"Going in the water," he said, still smiling, but sounding more his old self. "And you're... helping me. The drum is yours, Deana. Think of me." His other hand grasped my arm as well, and then he reached up and patted my head.

Then he faced the water, and I'll be damned if he didn't stand straight. "When Yareli and I are done, she will come to your home. Be out back, on the canal."

"What? Why? What are you talking about?"

"I am sorry I didn't know this before, Deana. I haven't seen my water lady for some time. But she came to me last night, and we were able to speak." The way he said 'my water lady' made the tears leak right out of my eyes as though they had a mind of their own. He took a step forward, and then another, his hand gripping my arm tightly. I helped him, and I could see that the woman in the water had lifted up her arms in a welcome.

We kept going to her. When the water was over my knees, we were close, and Caleb kneeled down and went into her arms.

"Caleb," she said, her voice low, musical in a way that fit with the song he'd just sung. Then she looked up at me, and smiled, but her teeth were sharp points. She was as scary as the vampires. "Thank you for bringing him to me."

"Sure," I said.

"Yareli will come to you," Caleb said, turning to look at me. "She has something to do first, but she will come to you. Go home, now, Deana. And wait."

"What are you going to do?" I asked.

"We will go," Yareli said, moving to put her arm around Caleb's shoulders and turn him toward the open ocean. Then she said something to him in a language I couldn't understand, and he smiled. His entire face glowed.

"Go," Yareli said to me. "We must go now. I will come later." She gave her smile again, and then towed Caleb further out.

I felt like I should be saying something, doing something, but this was obviously planned, and Caleb had smiled more than once in a way I'd never seen him smile. I watched as she carefully swam with him, and he let his head lie on her shoulder in one of the most tender things I'd ever seen. I watched as they swam out further, and further, their heads hard to see among the waves, and the setting sun.

Then they disappeared. And the tears flowed freely.

CHAPTER SIXTEEN

How long I stood there, looking at the now-empty ocean, I didn't know. But then I remembered—Caleb had told me to go home, and wait by the canal. I ran back to Baby, and was lucky I didn't get a ticket on the way home.

When I came racing through the kitchen, worried I'd missed Yareli, I saw that Tuesday was up.

"Hey, what's going on?" she asked.

"Come out on the deck with me, and don't talk. Afterwards, I'll tell you everything, but not right now."

One thing I'll say for Tuesday, she didn't ask a lot of questions when things needed to be done. She followed me, and I went out on the deck, and then down to the gate that led to our small landing on the canal. I sat down, and waited.

"What are we doing?" Tuesday asked.

"Waiting," I said.

"Okay."

The night was still, with only a few birds still flying over, making small noises of settling in for the night. The water was calm, and then I heard a slap, like someone was paddling. Then another, and I looked down the canal.

Something was coming toward us. I'd bet my NoMo spray it was the water lady. But I didn't move, or say anything.

"What is that?" Tuesday whispered.

"A friend. Maybe," I whispered back.

Yareli swam into view. Now I could see that she had a tail. Holy shit.

"Is Caleb all right?" I asked, not sure how to ask.

"He has moved on," she said, smiling. Her sharp teeth glinted in the moonlight. I felt, rather than saw, Tuesday's start at the teeth. They were the sort of teeth that a shark would envy, but they were thin, and needle sharp.

"Take care of him," I said.

"I shall," she inclined her head.

I was glad to know that I hadn't offended her.

"Caleb told me of your search. And that you must have answers at the next moonrise. Is that so?" Her accent was like nothing I'd ever heard before.

"Yes," I said.

"Then at the next moonrise, I shall be here. I shall share my story with those who need to hear it. You will bring them here?" She reached out of the water to touch my shoe.

I will never be able to describe what I felt when she touched me. It was like I'd stuck a fork in a light socket (which I did when I was young because I wanted my hair to be curlier, and someone told me in second grade that was how you got it), and yet it didn't hurt, but felt... wonderful. My descriptions, however, didn't do it justice.

"I will. You know what—who—I am looking for?" I asked hardly daring to believe what I was hearing, and hardly able to focus because in her touch I felt the open ocean, and riding the waves in the moon with a silence around me that was like singing.

She removed her hand, making a circle in the water. "I know what you are looking for. I will return and share that. I will even share of my blood, for the truth."

"Why?" I asked.

"You helped Caleb," she said. "That is important."

"I wanted to," I said.

"Who is—" Tuesday began, but I elbowed her and she didn't finish her question.

"Next moonrise," Yareli said again, and then she ducked under the water. I looked for her, but I didn't see her. I heard the slap of her tail in the distance.

"Wow," Tuesday said. "For someone who claims not to know a great deal about the witchy side of your family, you get around. Was that really a *mermaid*?"

"I think so. She didn't tell me anything about herself. Caleb called her the water lady."

"Who's Caleb?"

"A client of mine. He passed away recently," I tried to keep my voice steady. "He came to me asking for help."

"What was he?"

"A Native American spirit," I said, not wanting to share more about him.

Tuesday nodded. "I find the spirits who come to the human world interesting."

"He was," I said, walking back to the house.

"So what's next?"

"Let's call Delgado, and Levi—and we have to tell Delgado that he can't bring anyone," I said.

"He'll never go for that."

"We'll tell him he gets to meet a mermaid," I replied. "You think that might interest him enough?"

"It might," she said thoughtfully. "Let's go call him now."

"Let me, please," I said. "Even if he's skeptical, he won't be able to resist what he thinks is my last ditch effort."

"You're learning," Tuesday said. "Very good, Deana."

I dialed his number. It didn't even ring once before he answered.

"Ms. Deana. I cannot tell you how delighted I am to hear from you. What news from the investigative world?"

"I have found the killer," I said.

"Really?" His voice changed. He was shocked.

I was right. That bastard. He didn't think I'd manage it. Well, suck on that, asshat. I couldn't stop the grin that crossed my face. He couldn't see me, anyway. "Yes. And I have secured a promise of verification like you were able to get from Kel."

"Really?" he asked again.

Alfonso Delgado hadn't been lost for words since I'd met him. I felt a deep and vicious satisfaction that he'd repeated himself twice already.

"Yes. You need to come here as soon as you wake tomorrow. My witness will be here at moonrise—that's her word, and I figure you know what she means—and you need to come alone."

"No."

"Yes. Otherwise, you will not get to hear from a mermaid."

He laughed then. "Are there really such things? Are you really so desperate?"

"Tell him," I handed the phone to Tuesday.

"I saw her," Tuesday said. "She is as Deana says."

I didn't know what he said, but it made Tuesday smile, too. This was a red letter night all around in the fuck you department. She handed the phone back.

"Yes?" I asked.

"I will be there. My men will wait in the car."

"Levi and Tuesday will be there. And you will be able to verify."

"We shall see," Delgado was no longer sounding smooth and delighted. "I will see you tomorrow at just before moonrise, Deana."

Oh, I wasn't Ms. Deana anymore? It was all I could do not to laugh in his ear. What a baby! A dangerous, temper-tantrum throwing baby, if I had to make a guess. This was not on his agenda for sure, and while I didn't think I'd need to spray him and run, perhaps I should consider leaving. Out of sight, out of mind, and all that. "I'll be waiting. At my home."

He hung up.

I looked at Tuesday and we both stood in the kitchen laughing so hard we cried. Her tears were pink, which was disconcerting. Finally, we were both able to talk.

"I must thank you," she said.

"For what?"

"This is far better than rending him to pieces. He'll be in pieces, and I won't have to lift a finger."

"Revenge is sweet, isn't it?" I grinned.

"Are you sure that the mermaid has the information you need?"

I nodded.

"How?"

"That I can't get into, but I'm sure. And hey, it's my life on the line, right?"

"True," Tuesday nodded. "We should call Levi."

"You can do that," I said, feeling shy. I didn't think encouraging my own thoughts was a good idea.

She gave me a look and took out her own phone. As she walked away from me, talking with Levi, I went into the family room and collapsed on the couch. For the first time since Kel had walked into my office, I felt I could breathe, that impending doom wasn't about to fall on my head.

Not that I was sure I'd escaped all manner of doom, but it didn't feel like it was going to happen no matter what.

Tuesday came back over. "Levi wants to know if he can share my area at the dawning. He's worried that Delgado will try something. He wants to be here before Delgado shows up."

I was touched. "Yeah, that would be great. Delgado's pissed. I get the feeling no one tells him no very often."

"Exactly," Tuesday said, walking away again. Then she came back, her call done. "He's on his way over. We will not let Delgado harm you. You're doing as you agreed to—"

"I didn't agree to shit. I was told what I'd be doing by that highhanded asshat!" My peace was gone instantly in a flash of anger.

"True. You were told. But you didn't shirk from it, and you are offering him what he said he must have."

"I hope it's enough," I said.

"It will be. If it is not, I shall rend him to pieces," her voice was flat and angry.

"Tuesday, even after I'm in the clear with Delgado,

I'm leaving," I said, surprising myself. Shit. I hadn't meant to say that.

"To where?" she asked.

"I have a place. Do you want to come with me?"

Her eyebrows went up. "You continue to surprise me, Deana Holliday."

"Is that a good or a bad thing?"

"I think mostly good. Why do you want me to come with you?"

"Because I don't think you're happy here, either, and you're going to be on the Delgado shit list, too. We'll both be off the Christmas card list, in fact."

She sat down on the couch. "I had not considered that, but you're right." From her, that entire sentence was high praise. "Will it be safe for me?"

"It's in the desert, and it's hot and bright as shit, but it's also in the middle of nowhere, so at night, it's nice and dark. And we'll make a place for you."

"What will you expect of me?"

"I don't get what you're asking," I said.

"I am not looking for another mate," Tuesday said bluntly.

"Uh, that wasn't my intention," I said, realizing instantly I needed to be as tactful as possible. "But I'd like to ask you to come as my friend. Nothing more."

She nodded, and then stared off at the wall. One thing I'd learned about her was that she could be very still, and it didn't do any good to rush her.

"I'd never considered leaving. I would need to talk to my leader," she said.

"Then go see him."

Tuesday stood up. "I'll be back before dawning." She left, and I heard the front door close.

I went behind her and locked it. Then I took my time, going around and locking all the doors and windows that wouldn't be needed tomorrow. Because I'd be leaving after Delgado left, and I didn't want to hang around in case he had plans for me.

Since I wasn't in a rush anymore, I went through the house again, making sure I had what I needed to start over. I had no idea what the place in Bisbee had as far as being able to live. It looked a little run down, but it was an old building with a garage, and that was the most important thing, in my opinion.

As I walked through the kitchen, I saw the our coffee machine. Actually, it made cappuccino, and expresso, and any manner of coffee drinks. It was gleaming copper, and I was pretty sure Mom would be pissed if I took it.

But I was headed out to the wild unknown, and coffee had sustained me this week. She would get over it if I promised to get her another one. I made the decision, and took my time dismantling it, then packing it carefully in the car.

Tomorrow I'd go to the office, and... I didn't know what I'd do. I'd worked so hard to get that place, and now, I was just walking away from it.

But my gut told me this was the thing to do. I hadn't chosen this. This mess had been foisted on me. However, I was done with other people making choices for me. I would leave, start over—thank you, Caleb— and keep the pact I'd made with him.

When I crawled into bed after a shower, I fell asleep easily.

CHAPTER SEVENTEEN

I WAS UP WITH THE SUN. THERE WERE TWO LARGE suitcases in my room with a note on top of them.

I didn't know what to do with these. Since I'm guessing our departure will be imminent, I am leaving them here for you. Please pack them with your things.

It wasn't signed. But Tuesday had made her decision, and that made me feel better.

After I got ready, I hauled her bags down to the car, and packed them. Then I covered everything in the back of Baby with the tonneau cover I'd had made for her cargo space. No need to advertise. I went to my office. I had to say goodbye. Even though it was going to suck. I could always come back to the house on Carroll Canal. But I would never come back here.

I went through carefully, like I had at home. I wanted to take all the things I needed, that I wanted. The furniture could stay. When I was done, I walked to the door, a box under my arm. It was just a small office with stinky carpet, and in a less than desirable location in a strip mall—but it had been mine.

And now it wasn't anymore. I'd sent an email to my landlord, told him to keep the deposit in order to clean it out. Thanks to the less than desirable location, he was used to places closing overnight. It had just never been in my plans for one of those places to be mine.

There was no sense in carrying on. I turned to open the door, and I was pushed back in by someone coming in. I fell backwards, knocking over one of the chairs in front of my desk before I landed on my ass.

"Hey, what the hell?" I yelled. Picking myself up, I prepared to kick some ass. And found myself facing the demon Madigan.

"What are you doing here?" I yelled. "I still have three weeks, give or take."

"While that is true," Madigan brushed non-existent lint from the arm that I thought had knocked me down, and pulled the chair I hadn't fallen into toward him, taking a seat, "It has come to my attention that the previous owner of the Volcanic is no more."

Jesus, Mary, and Joseph. I made my face as mean and ugly as I could, so as to not give away my shock that he already knew. How did he know? What kind of gossip network did the demons have? "So you're firing me?" I asked.

"No, not at all. I want you to find it. In fact, I think

you have it, Deana Holliday. And you're going to give it to me."

"I don't have it. I've been dealing with some other cases that had some precedence and you were next on the list."

"Yes, I heard. Rather interesting to think you didn't even know your family history a month ago, and now you're on the radar of people who are doing their level best to turn you, control you, or kill you, don't you think?"

"No, I don't find it interesting at all. I'm not interested in any of those people, and I wish they'd get the hell out of my life!" I glared so hard at him I thought I might burst a blood vessel in my eyeballs.

The smug piece of shit *laughed*. "You are so wonderful, really. I almost hate to be here in my current capacity."

"And what is that?" If I gritted my teeth any harder, I'd grind them to bits. Then at least I'd have something good to spit at him before I died. I wondered if I could get to the NoMo spray in my pocket. I wasn't sure. He struck me as fast. Like a rattlesnake.

Who looked better than he should in a suit. But at least if I spit, his suit would get dirty. That was a pleasant thought.

"As a disgruntled client. Now, I am in fact a client. I did hire you—"

"No, you told me what you wanted. I don't recall getting a choice in the matter," I said.

"Well, no, you didn't. And that's fine. I don't give choices when I need something done. And what I need is that Volcanic." Like the rattlesnake I'd compared him to a minute ago, he was up and gripping the neck of my jacket hard, nearly lifting me off my feet. "So now we're going to go to your safe, and you're going to open it up, and then I'll go from being a disgruntled client to a satisfied client. I might even go away." He moved around the desk, frog-marching me along with him.

We walked down the back hallway, and he shoved me into the back office. "Open the safe, Deana."

"No."

He hit me. I flew into the futon, and I heard the frame break. Good thing I'd decided to leave the furniture.

"Open the safe, Deana."

"Can't you and your magic fire hands open it?" I asked, remembering Asher.

"While I imagine you fancy yourself a demon expert, we're not all the same. And I am making you open the safe because I want you to, Deana. I want to see you open it, and give it to me."

I got up, brushing myself off, and felt blood on the side of my head. Asshat. Moving carefully, because I wasn't going to pat myself down in front this douchenozzle, I kneeled down at the safe. Opening it, I stood. "Have a look."

"Give me the pistol."

"For the bazillionth time, I do not have it. Please, take a look for yourself."

He rushed to the safe, and began pulling things out of it. I'd left a stack of twenties in there, and they went flying. Two bank bags, and there was nothing else in there.

"Where is it?" Madigan stood up, his eyes blazing. They were taking on a distinct shade of red.

"I wish to hell I knew. Because then maybe you'd get out of my office, and my life," I shot back.

"You know where it is."

"I don't even know what it is," I said. "It's not just a pistol. I guessed that. But you didn't give me anything else, and do you know how many there are for sale? More than one. I'm not spending money I don't have on your wild goose chase. Money you just threw all over the room, I might add," I gestured to the money on the floor. "Thanks for that, by the way."

His eyes shone brightly. "The money on the floor is the least of your worries. I'm not going to kill you, because I do like you, and I also think you're going to end up giving me the pistol. I always win, Deana. Always. I have all the time in the world. As you're not in Deadwood, unfortunately, you do not." He brushed himself off, pulled down the vest of his suit, and turned on his heel, stalking from the room.

I hurried after him. "Leave me alone, Madigan! I can't help you, and I'm firing you as a client!" I yelled the last bit at his back.

Madigan stopped at the door, turned around, and said something I couldn't understand, and my office burst into flames. Then he yelled something, and the wall to my right fell down. He opened the door, and shouted, and I felt the whole building shake. It knocked me to the ground.

He walked through the flames. "And I keep my word, Deana Holliday. You aren't shut down. You're just... mostly closed." He looked around, tugged at his vest again. "At least they'll think it's an act of God," he laughed at that last word. "And you can get some money for this dump. Make up for the twenties on the floor, wouldn't you say? No, no, don't get up," he held a hand out to me as I got to my knees. "I'll see myself out. I'll be seeing you, Deana."

Stepping through the flames again, he disappeared. Leaving me to struggle to my feet, and hop around the flames that were steadily growing larger. I gathered up the box that I'd been carrying when Madigan came in, and limped into the parking lot.

It took longer than I was happy about to get through the questions about the fire, and talk to the police. Thankfully, everyone else in the strip mall had gotten out, and no one was seriously hurt. I was the worst off, but I didn't tell them that was because a demon had tossed me around.

The paramedics treated the cuts on my face, told me to ice the bruises, and then let me go. After making sure the cops were done with me, and calling my insurance company, I went home. They were sending an adjustor out today, so hopefully I could wrap that up before I had to go sometime tomorrow. Otherwise, it would look like I'd done something wrong. I needed no more loose ends than I already had.

Once home, I prowled around restlessly. I checked and re-checked Baby, and the trailer I'd bought. I hooked and unhooked the trailer, so I knew that I could get it done up fast.

Then I called the insurance company again, and told them that I'd come home because I was tired. They surprised me by asking if the adjustor could come by.

"Sure. That was fast," I said.

"You're not the only one who had to have someone out there," the woman on the other end said. "Can he stop by?"

"Absolutely."

Within the hour, the adjustor was ringing the doorbell. I let him in. A man of medium height, middle age, and a very sunny disposition came in, introducing himself. "I'm Ken Bateman, Miss Holliday. I'm very sorry about your business. Are you all right?" He peered at my head and face, which admittedly didn't look all that hot.

"I don't feel great, for a lot of reasons, but the EMTs told me it was superficial."

"Well, that's good. Can we sit down somewhere?"

"Sure, come into the kitchen. Can I get you a drink?"

"Water would be great. It's pretty hot over at the strip mall."

"What caused the fire? Do they know?"

He shook his head. "The fire chief thinks it was a gas line, and that's what caused the whole place to suffer."

An act of God, Madigan had said. Well, maybe I wouldn't be a suspect. That would be nice. Not that I was feeling grateful towards the prick. I gave Ken the glass of water, and sat down to see what he had to say.

Ken Bateman and I talked for nearly an hour, and he left, setting his card on my kitchen table. "I think that's all I'll need, Deana. If I need anything else, I'll call. But I spoke with some of the other adjustors, and while this is a mess, and I am sorry for you, I don't think this will be overly complicated. Especially if the Chief's report is a reflection of his thoughts today. May I call you if I need to?"

"Of course. You have my number," I said. I didn't tell him that I'd be out of the state. If he did call, I could tell him I was traveling.

I saw him out the door, and went out to sit on the deck. The canal was calm, as it usually was, and there were a few people out on their kayaks. Their voices carried softly across the water. I closed my eyes and let my head tilt back after touching my front pocket to make sure the NoMo spray was easily accessible.

When the sun got too much to bear, I went inside, and checked everything yet again. Then I called my mom.

"Deana," she said.

"Listen, Mom, I've burned the pans. I'm really sorry, I didn't mean to, but I was cooking, and got distracted."

She didn't respond right away, but then said, "Well, then you'll need to replace them. When do you think you can get them?" She'd remembered our conversation about me possibly needed to get out of here.

"I'll head out tomorrow to see if I can find the set," I answered.

"Did you get the body spray we sent? I really loved the smell of it."

"I did, thank you. You guys are so good to me."

"I love you, sweetie. I'm just glad you're okay. Burning up the pans is no big loss as long you're all right."

"I'm a little shaken, but I'll be okay. I just wanted to let you know," I said.

"All right. Well, take care, honey. Try and get the same brand."

"I'm cheaper than you, Mom. But I'll try."

"Love you," she said.

"Love you," I replied.

Then we hung up.

I checked over the house again. The only doors I'd need to manage if I had to leave quickly were the front and back doors. Everything else was locked down.

"Oh, shit," I said out loud. The attorney. I went out to the garage and dug out Caleb's papers. Martin Dovetree. I called him, and he was obviously an old man.

"Your grandfather was such a nice man," he said. "He gave you everything you need except the keys."

"The keys?" I asked, feeling stupid. My grandfather?

"Yes, I have a ring of keys for you. He said you'd know what to do with them. When do you want to come and get them?"

"Would now be all right?"

"Sure."

I raced over to see him, making sure I had my NoMo spray, and a fire tea bag in my pocket. Since this was Caleb's deal, I didn't think I'd need them, but you never know. The past week had shown me that.

When I got there, Martin Dovetree was in fact, an old man. He was also Native American, and I wondered if that was why Caleb had chosen him. He shook my hand, patting the top of it with his other hand.

"All the paperwork is in order. You should have no problems, but if you do, you have my card. I just need you to sign for the keys," he said, pulling out a large, old-fashioned ring that had a bunch of keys on it, some old, some modern. He set them on his desk, and then took out a file, and opened it, handing it to me with a pen. I signed, and gave it back.

"I was sorry to hear of his illness."

"There was nothing that could be done," I said. "But he was peaceful to the end."

"You were with him?"

I nodded. "I drummed for him," I said, figuring he'd understand.

He did. A smile crossed his face. "Good luck to you, Miss Holliday."

"Thank you," I said. A thought struck me. "Do you speak Cree?"

"A little. Don't you?"

"No, I didn't know he was my... grandfather until recently," I said. "What does *câpân* mean?"

A look of surprise replaced the smile. "It means, loosely translated, great-grandfather, and great-grandchild."

Tears filled my eyes.

"You didn't know?"

I shook my head, unable to speak. How had this man I'd known such a short time touched me so deeply?

"Well, now you do," Mr. Dovetree said kindly.

"Thank you," I got out. I put the keys in my pocket and drove him, mopping my eyes the entire way. Once I was home, there was nothing more to do, so I fidgeted and pretended to watch TV until the sun was setting. I thought about Caleb. I wished I could see him again. As the sun began to set, I brushed my tears away, washed my face, and got ready for tonight's show. I figured there would be fireworks of some kind.

The moment the sky went dark, Tuesday and Levi came out into the living room.

"He's not here, is he?" Levi asked.

"No, you guys beat him. Thank god. I'm glad you're both here," I said.

"So are we. He won't hurt you, Deana," Tuesday said. "But someone did. What happened?"

I explained that my building had suffered a major gas explosion. For the time being, I didn't mention Madigan. For whatever reason, I felt I needed to keep that to myself.

"It's good you're not badly hurt," Tuesday said, eying my cuts.

"They look worse than they are." I shrugged, wanting to end the conversation.

"You don't suspect any foul play?" Levi asked.

There was a whole heaping shitful of foul play, but I wasn't going to get into it. In order not to lie outright, I merely shook my head.

"Chicks dig scars," Tuesday deadpanned.

Which made me smile.

Levi brought us back on track. "As long as this information is good," Levi added. "You feel confident in your informant?"

I nodded.

"Well, hopefully Delgado's on time. I don't get the feeling that—what was her name?" Tuesday asked.

"Yareli," I said. "The water lady."

"I don't get the impression she'll wait."

The doorbell rang, and Levi went to answer it. He came in with Delgado on his heels.

"My men are in the car, and I have my phone on, so they can hear everything. If you attempt to cross me, Deana Holliday—"

Oh, now I was First Name Last Name? I'd bet my ass I wasn't welcome in the harem at all anymore.

"Then they shall hear it, and none of you will survive." His voice was loaded with menace. "What happened to your face?"

"I'm not the one who threatened people in the first place," I said. "All I did was work for my client." I shrugged. "You're not in danger. My face was hurt when there was a gas explosion at my office. Come on, let's go wait for her."

It was crowded on the canal landing. I sat down, crossing my legs. Looking up, I said, "You all might as well relax. She'll be here, and you'll be able to hear her better if you're sitting."

Tuesday took a seat next to me, and Levi sat behind me.

Delgado remained standing, looking at how they'd surrounded me. Then with a noise of disgust, he sat down on the other end of the landing. "You seem to experiencing a serious case of bad luck, Deana."

"Shit happens," I said.

He glared, about to say something, probably something shady and snarky, but I held up a hand.

I could hear the slight splash down the canal. "Shhh," I said. "She's coming."

CHAPTER EIGHTEEN

I NOTICED THAT ALL THREE OF THE VAMPIRES LEANED forward.

The sounds of someone swimming got closer, and I felt my heart beat faster. Then before I expected it, she was at the landing and reaching up to touch my leg. The jolt I'd felt when she touched me last night raced through me, and I was filled with an exhilaration that things would be all right.

I didn't care if it was just a pick me up on her part, because it felt amazing.

"I am here to offer witness to the death of a vampire on the beach half a moon cycle ago," Yareli said. "Where are those who are to bear witness to me?"

"I am here," Delgado said.

"And so are we," Tuesday said.

"There are three of you?" Yareli looked over all of us on the landing. Her eyes landed on me last, and I noticed that they were gleaming gold in the moonlight. I nodded.

She lifted up her hand, and bit the fleshy side of it. "You may each have a few drops of my blood." She offered it first to Tuesday, then Levi, and last to Delgado, swimming to get closer to him.

"I shall tell you what I saw, Deana Holliday. I was close to the beach that night, out at the large point."

I assumed she meant Point Duma, and I nodded.

"I became alarmed when I saw the woman with the flapping garment on the beach, because I could sense that she was not human. So I moved away. But then I saw something moving down the cliff, and I stopped to watch. Watching the world above the waves is a past time of mine. I never know what I might see," she said, looking at me, and I knew she meant Caleb.

I nodded again, not willing to interrupt.

Next to me, all three of the vampires gasped. I looked at them. Their eyes were closed, and they all had varying expression of pleasure on their faces. If her touch affected me as it did, what would her blood do?

"The figure from the cliffs came down to the beach. I swam in closer, and I could see then that he had a glow of one not of this world. Even hooded and covered, I could see him."

"What do you mean?" Delgado got out with difficulty.

"He was not of the earth. He was not of the water. He came from the land of the dead, below the ground."

"Hell," I said.

"Yes, the land of the dead," Yareli repeated. "He walked closer and closer to the woman, and she turned, surprised. He put his hands around her neck, and his glow brightened, a dark red, like the red around the moon at times." She stopped.

"She tried to fight, striking at him with her arms, and legs. But he was too strong, and as his glow brightened, her attempts to fight him off became smaller, weaker."

Levi gave a strangled sound behind me.

"She fell to the sand, and the figure in the hood stood over her for a time, and then he walked a distance away from her, and he disappeared. That is what I saw, and this is my truth." She stopped.

There was silence all around me. Not even the water dared to take a breath.

Then Levi spoke, leaning over the landing to look at Yareli. "I thank you for sharing how my mate was killed."

She inclined her head regally.

"Do you concur now that you have an idea of the killer's identity, and that Deana Holliday has fulfilled the agreement between you?" Tuesday's voice cut through the evening like a knife.

I resisted the urge to bitch about the use of the word agreement.

Delgado didn't answer right away. Shit. We were going to have to fight out way out.

"He cannot deny my truth," Yareli interjected. "Is what you saw as I described?" she asked Delgado.

"You did not give me the name," Delgado said.

"There was no name to give. But I have allowed you to see that it was a demon who killed her," I objected. I got up, letting my hands slip down to my pockets. The NoMo spray first—the fire tea bag would bring his men in here running. They were a little noisy.

"You are very close to not upholding your word," Levi said.

Delgado looked at Levi, and in that look, I saw him judging whether continuing on would be worth the hassle. Then he looked away. "Deana Holliday, I agree that you have fulfilled our agreement," Delgado said grudgingly, his teeth clicking as he shut his mouth tightly.

Apparently *not* worth it. Now I had to resist the urge to laugh in his face. I knew—or at least, I had an idea—of how much it cost him to say that.

"Then you need to leave," Levi said. "Tuesday, let's show Alfonso out, and reassure his men that all is well." He got up, and he and Tuesday placed themselves between me and Delgado.

The three of them left without another word. When I heard the door to the deck close, I leaned down to Yareli. "Thank you. Thank you so much. You saved me."

"You eased Caleb's passing. I am grateful to you. I was pleased that Caleb told me there was something I could do to show my gratitude. We are now equal with one another."

"He's all right?" I asked.

She smiled, and in that smile, I saw the same look I'd seen on Caleb's face as he walked into the water with her. "He is all right. He will see you again. Be well, Deana Holliday."

Then she slipped beneath the water, and I didn't even hear a splash to announce her leaving.

I sat on the landing for a long time, watching the moon on the water. Finally, I got up and went back to face whatever was waiting for me inside.

When I came in, Tuesday and Levi were waiting for me.

"Did you see everything she described?"

"And then some," Tuesday said. "Are you going to be okay, Levi?"

He rubbed at his eyes, and I saw pink around them. "It was difficult seeing it, but I thank you for making it possible for me to see, Deana. A demon killed her. So her shorthand did mean demon. And that means Delgado knows something about the demons. Maybe even this one."

"Don't go after him now," I said.

"I will not. But I will discover the connection, and if Delgado had anything to do with this, he will wish I killed him quickly." The menace in Levi's voice reverberated through the room.

"You should go home," Tuesday said. "Go and feed, and then go home."

His expression was shuttered and dark, but he nodded. "Thank you, to both of you." He turned and left.

Tuesday looked at me. "What now?"

"Do you need to feed?"

"I should. But the mermaid's blood," her eyes took a dreamy look, "Was incredible. I feel I could walk in the sun now."

"She touched me. That's what her touch feels like."

"I've never tasted anything like it before." She stared off in the distance, her expression still dreamy. Then she snapped to me. "We will need to leave. Levi won't rest until Delgado is either implicated or cleared. This is how wars begin."

"Christ, that wasn't what I was trying to do," I said.

"It's our way," Tuesday shrugged. "You do not bear any responsibility for that. I think I will go and feed, and then when will we leave?"

"Tonight. So we can get somewhere and get you a hidey hole before the sun comes up."

"I will be quick." She zipped from the room and I heard the click of the door. We'd need to come to some sort of agreement about her feeding once we got to Bisbee. People couldn't be dropping every seven days, or whatever her feeding schedule was. But that was under the heading of future business.

I hitched up the trailer to Baby, and went through

the house again. I'd miss it. But I didn't have time to mourn just yet. Pulling up the map, I looked to see how far we could get if Tuesday was back in two hours.

It would take us ten hours to get to Bisbee. So I chose a place right in the middle—Yuma, Arizona. I was taking the more rural route, and I booked two nights at a vacation rental in an RV park. The RV was dark, with good blackout curtains. I figured Tuesday and I could sleep all day, and then get up at night, and make our way to Bisbee. Two nights would cover us for however long we needed to be there. Then we'd be able to reach the house that Caleb had left me, and I figured I'd be able to find her somewhere. There had to be a cellar in that thing. It had the look.

Tuesday was back in under an hour.

"That was quick," I said, feeling a little alarm.

"I do not need to feed from one person only. I take a sip here, a sip there, and I move through a crowd quickly, so that no one notices."

I burst out laughing in relief.

"What's so funny?"

"I was thinking about how we had to have a conversation that you couldn't be killing all over the place where we're going. It's a lot smaller than Los Angeles."

She gave me a dirty look. "There is no need to kill at all. It's messy, and complicated."

"Somehow, I don't think all your kind feel the same way."

"No, you're right. Some are stuck in the past. But

they are not the ones who last. Are we leaving? What else is there to do?"

"Nothing. I've got everything packed, even your stuff. All we need to do is leave."

She looked at me, and then said, "You were preparing to do this no matter what?"

I nodded.

"Even before you had the proof from the mermaid?"

A little more slowly, I nodded again.

"You continue to surprise me, Deana."

"Is that a good thing?"

She laughed. "It is. Let's go."

We drove away, and I looked in my rear view mirror. I'd miss it, but I felt a sense of excitement that I hadn't felt in a long time. I wondered what kind of pie I'd be called to bake once we got to Bisbee. I'd need to start keeping pie crusts in the freezer, just in case. Would it be a pie for everyone? Or just the person who started whatever it was I was going to be dealing with? It was something to think about.

We drove through the night, occasionally talking. I finally mustered up the courage to ask Tuesday something that had been nagging at me. "What did Zachary say when you told him you wanted to leave?"

"He did not release me from my ties to him," she said. "But he agreed that my leaving Los Angeles could be good for me. When I told him I would be with you, I think that sealed his decision. He's interested in you."

"Yeah, like a commodity."

"That's true, but you're aware of it. It doesn't have to be a negative thing. Knowledge of something allows it to be used as a weapon."

"Tuesday, my knowledge of things nearly got me killed. More than once, probably."

"Yes, but that was before you understood. Now you do. I shall help you. You will not need to be at the mercy of men like Delgado again."

"I'd appreciate that," I said honestly. "I am usually at the mercy of no one, and I don't like it."

"Where did you get the bikes?" she asked, changing the subject.

I sighed. Fair was fair, I supposed. I told her the whole long tale of Derek, and then my falling out with Kel, and how the bikes came to me.

"He is a weak man," she said.

"I'd agree with you partly. But he did his best to make amends."

"If you say so. While the bikes are beautiful, I'm not sure they were worth the hassle."

"Oh, they were," I said definitively. "They were."

She was silent, then asked, "Will you teach me to ride them?"

"You don't know how?"

She shook her head. "I've never had the chance. But I can see why you like it, and I'd like to learn."

"Sure," I said, oddly pleased by her request. "I'm glad you decided to come with me."

LISA MANIFOLD

"I thank you for asking me. Zachary was right. I needed to leave."

I smiled, and we didn't talk anymore. We got to the RV camp around three, and I followed the instructions I'd gotten from the owner. When we came in, Tuesday looked around approvingly. "This is dark enough that I will be safe."

"That was my thought, too. Let's get some sleep."

We shared the one bed, after making sure that the blackout curtains were tightly closed, and snapped down.

"You're not worried to be sharing a space with me?" Tuesday asked.

"Where else would you sleep? On the floor? In the bathroom?"

"I have my sleeping bag," she said.

"No, I'm not scared," I said.

I couldn't read the expression on Tuesday's face, but I lay down in bed, rolling over. I had the NoMo spray under my pillow, just in case. I didn't know if vampires dreamed, or if they were completely still, but just in case, it was there.

I woke first, and it was late in the day. I got up, and went out into the front of the RV, making sure to close the door behind me so no light would get in. I showered, and made some coffee. I hadn't even thought of bringing food, but I figured once Tuesday was up, we could stop somewhere along the way and roll through a drive through. Now all I wanted was to get to Bisbee.

What would I do there? I wanted to open another business, to have roots in the place, so I looked like I had a reason to be there. A thought came to me, and I pulled out my laptop.

There was an email from Ken Bateman, informing me the insurance company would be issuing me a check for the loss of my business. He also said that any other business I chose to insure with them would require a few extra steps, now that they'd had to pay out. I wrote back and asked him if we could do a direct deposit. That would solve me having to offer any more information. I also told him I was considering my options, which included relocating outside of LA, since I was understandably nervous after the accident.

Then I turned my attention to my original thought, and as I looked at options, and then, placed an order, and asked for it to be rushed, I found that I was smiling from ear to ear.

It was dark when Tuesday came out. "Are you ready to leave?"

"Just about. What do you need to do?"

"Nothing. We can leave when you wish to."

I gathered up my things, emailed the owner to let him know we were leaving, and within twenty minutes, we were on the road. We'd been driving for about an hour when my mom's ringtone sounded through the car.

"Hey," I said.

"Oh, my goddess, Deana, are you all right?"

"What do you mean, Mom?"

"I just got a call from the police," she said, and then she burst into tears.

"Mom, what happened? What's going on?"

I heard some shuffling, and then the phone clicked.

"Deana, you're on speaker." It was Daniella.

"Hang on, I think I need to pull over," I said. I handed the phone to Tuesday, and pulled off to the side of the road. I hooked the phone into its holder, and hit the speaker button. "Okay, I'm back. What's happened?"

"The house in Venice is gone," Gran said. I could tell she'd been crying. "The police called, and told us it was on fire, and it burned to the ground."

"What?" I whispered.

Tuesday was about to say something, but I put my hand on her arm to stop her.

"How?" I asked.

"They don't know," Gran said. "They told us they couldn't tell if anyone was in there. Dee told us about your call the other day, but she didn't know the details. Are you all right?"

"That utter bastard," I said.

"Who?" It sounded like all five of them shouted.

"Alfonso Delgado. This is his doing. I'd bet Baby on it."

"You're that sure?" Mom said.

"Who is Baby?" Desdemona asked.

"My car," I said. "My wonderful car, which was not

in the house when it blew up. No, I'm not there. I am on the road, and I'll let you know where I am a little later."

"Are you on the run?" Deirdre asked.

I was pleased to see that she grasped the situation immediately. "Apparently so. I thought it would be a good idea to get the hell out of Dodge, so to speak, since I thwarted the plans of Delgado, but now he's upped the stakes."

"You know," Desdemona said. "We might be able to buy you some time."

"How?" Mom and Gran asked together.

"Now that we know you're safe, you get to wherever. We'll call you back when we have some idea of whether this can work," Desdemona said. "Stay safe, Deana."

"Love you," I said.

"Love you," came a chorus through the phone.

When I hung up, I looked at Tuesday. "This must be his way of attempting to regain control of the situation."

"He knew I was staying with you," she said.

"Well, you're a thorn in his ass, too."

"That son of a bitch," she hissed.

"Do you need to call Zachary?"

"Well," she picked up her phone. Then she set it down. "No. Let them think I burned. It will be more heat on him, in the long run."

"He hasn't called you?"

"No. But you know, we should call Levi."

"Will he keep this under wraps?"

"He hates Delgado now," she said. "He wasn't a fan before, but he hates him now."

"Call him, then."

"You want to get going again?"

I shook my head, knowing she could see me even in the dark. "No. Let him think that we're just somewhere else. No need for him to know we're still in transit."

She dialed his number.

"Tuesday! Are you well?" He sounded excited.

His accent thickened when he was excited. The thought brought a flush to my face. I really needed to get my girl crush on this guy—vampire—under control.

"I am."

"Where is Deana?"

"She is with me."

"You both are safe?"

"We are. We felt that we needed to remove ourselves from public view for a time."

"It's a good thing you did. Is Deana there now?"

"Yes," I said.

"I'm sorry about your home, Deana. But I'm very glad you both are all right."

"We are."

"Where are you?"

"Safe and somewhere else," I said before Tuesday could answer. "Does everyone think we were still there?"

"Yes," he said. "I got a call from Delgado himself."

"I'm sure you did," anger dripped from my voice.

"Can you please not tell anyone any different, if everyone thinks we were in the house?"

"With pleasure," Levi said. "Contact me when you get to where you're going." He hung up.

"He's going to kick Delgado's ass," Tuesday said.

"Well, he deserves it. That house was unique. It was special."

"But you're still alive," Tuesday said. "That's the important thing."

I sat with shaking hands, then as they started to calm, I laughed out loud.

"Are you losing it?" Tuesday asked. "I can drive if you need to have a breakdown."

"No," I said, between laughing. "I'm laughing because I'll bet you money that my mom will be calling me and lamenting about the cappuccino machine."

"It is a really nice machine," Tuesday said. "While I no longer drink coffee, I enjoyed the scent of it being made."

"I have it," I said, laughing harder. "I took it, and I was debating how I was going to make it up to my mom and Gran, because we all love that thing."

She laughed with me, and finally, I was able to start the car and get back on the road. Delgado was going to pay. Between spinning fantasies in my head about how to make that come to pass, I wondered what my aunts were planning.

CHAPTER NINETEEN

WE PULLED INTO BISBEE A LITTLE AFTER TWO IN THE morning. I drove slowly, looking around. This was my new home.

"I feel like a gunfighter is about to step out and start shooting," Tuesday said.

"You watch too many movies," I chuckled. "This is a nice, respectable tourist town. They focus on art and creativity now. We'll fit right in."

That made her laugh. "Perhaps you will."

"No, you will as well. It's one of the reasons I asked you. There's a funky vibe here that I think will make it easy for you to blend in. Here, you'll just be eccentric."

"What are you going to do?"

"I'm going to reopen my place. Maybe under a different name, though."

"Why?"

"I'm not going to advertise my own name."

"Probably a good call," she agreed. My GPS told me we were there, and I looked over to the left. There it was, just as it looked in the pictures.

Well, maybe a little worse for wear.

"This is a far cry from your previous home," Tuesday said. "I think you'll need to do some work on it."

"Maybe, but it has the important thing," I said. I went up the street to make a u-turn, and then came and parked on the sidewalk. Taking out the bundle of keys I'd gotten from the attorney, I sifted through them until I found one that looked like it matched the garage lock.

"Would have been nice to have labels," I muttered.

"I could just break it," Tuesday offered.

"No. I want to use the lock after we get the car in there."

I had to try a couple of keys until I found the right one. When I opened the doors, I saw that the garage when all the way through the building.

"Let's get the trailer unhooked. I think we can back it in ourselves," I said.

"I could probably do it on my own," Tuesday said.

"Oh, right. All the strength." Duh. "Well, good. "Let's get them in, and then we can pull the car in."

I unhitched the trailer, and Tuesday lifted it up. "You'll need to move your car. This won't be a problem."

I pulled forward, and before I'd even gotten out of the car, she had it backed in. I inspected her work—she was good. "There's plenty of room for Baby," I said happily. "Let's get her in, and then we can unload her."

I backed Baby in. "Well, why don't we check out the new digs?"

Tuesday looked dubious, but she nodded. I had a feeling she was reserving judgement. That was all right with me—I loved it. It reminded me—albeit with more dust and in dire need of a good cleaning, maybe two or three—of Deadwood. To me, that was a good thing. It wasn't the house on Pearl Street, but I could make it my own.

"There's a door back here," Tuesday called out.

"What?"

"There's a door back here. Why don't we see if it leads indoors? Then we can close the garage and move things in peace."

This time, it took a little more testing to find the right key. "I'm going to need to label these things," I grumbled.

"I think that would be a good idea," Tuesday said. She was covering a smile.

"Shut up," I said. "Nobody needs your commentary right now."

We walked in, and we were on a landing. Straight ahead was the ground floor, and to our right was a staircase leading down. "I knew this would have a cellar," I said.

"That's important?"

"I thought it would be a safe place for your room."

I was gratified to see a look of pleasure on her face. "Shall we see if I need to evict anyone first?"

"Sure." I turned on the flashlight on my phone, and we walked down the stairs. There was just enough room to stand up, and the far wall was lined with shelves. There were a lot of canned goods. "Oh, eww. I wonder how long those have been there? We'll need to go through them. That looks like botulism city."

"There's room for a bed, and a dresser," Tuesday said.

"There's also another room in the back," I pointed to a doorway that was blacker than night. Moving closer, I shined my flashlight through it. "It's a bathroom." Peering around the doorway, we could see a commode and a narrow shower.

"This is perfect," Tuesday said happily.

"Is it?"

"I have not had my own dwelling since I became vampire," she said.

Oh. Well. I didn't know what to say to that. "Well, this is all yours. We'll definitely fix it up for you so you're comfortable."

"Let's go see the rest."

Heading back up the stairs, the ground floor had obviously been used as some kind of office. Which was fricken perfect. There was even a large window in the front where my sign could hang. The thought made me smile.

Past the landing where we'd entered, there was

another stairway that led to the second story, and that was set up as a small apartment.

"This definitely needs updating," Tuesday said, her nose wrinkling.

"Yeah, but that's fun."

"Did you buy this sight unseen?" She asked.

"It was a gift," I said, not willing to go any further.

"I suppose it is a gift."

"Snotty!" I laughed. "It's not that bad."

My cell rang, and I saw that it was Desdemona calling.

"Hey," I said.

"We have contacted some... friends. They've put a body in the ruins. Didn't you tell me that a vampire was sleeping there? Where was she?"

"In the old wine cellar area."

"I can make sure there's some clothing, and something that will alert the vamps that someone was there. No problem. Are you safe?"

"We are. We may die of dust or botulism, but we're safe for the moment."

"I'm dying to ask for more info, but I think I'll refrain," she said. "I'm glad you're okay, Deana. Your mom is sleeping, or I'd let you talk to her. She's been worried."

"She's been right to, but I think I've sorted it. You adding a body will make things even better. But—"

"What?"

"You didn't go out and get a body, did you?"

"Yes, but it was a body that was already gone before anything like this happened. We'll throw a big funeral for you. It will be epic."

"That feels weird," I said.

"Well, I don't doubt it. But the longer that vamp thinks you're dead, the better it is for you. We might even fly out for the funeral."

"Don't," I said. "That will make you too vulnerable. And I would venture a guess that my enemies are now your enemies. Why don't you have the body flown to Deadwood? Bury me in the family plot that Granny bought?"

"What a good idea," she said. "We can really do it up that way, and no one is going to mess with us here."

"Are Mom and Gran going to stay with you?" I asked, getting to something that had been worrying me since I'd heard about the canal house.

"Yes. They're dithering right now, but this is the best place for them. They just haven't accepted it yet. They are going to need time to mourn."

"I'm glad they're with you."

"We'll take care of them. And of you, Deana."

"Thank you," I said, feeling the tears welling in my eyes. I'd cried more in the last two weeks than I had since Derek died. "Hey, quick question. Why is there a zombie in the basement of the shop?"

Tuesday glanced over at my words.

"Oh, these things happen." Desdemona was breezy. "It's not the big deal your mom is making it out to be."

"Maybe not for you," I said.

"That's true. But look, they're already settling in. DeAnna even cusses at least once a day."

"Good. She needs to loosen up."

"I have a favor to ask."

"What, like getting a body double for you wasn't enough? Take, take, take. Kids these days," she said mockingly.

"Can you find out more about my great grandfather?"

"DeAnna's father?"

"Yes."

"I can, but why?"

"Because I have it on fairly good authority that he wasn't quite human?"

"Really?" Desdemona's voice sharpened.

"Yes."

"What is he?"

"The suspect was leaning toward the Ashlar type."

Desdemona was silent. "Well, that wasn't what I was expecting. Damn you, Deana. Not you," she hastened to add. "The first one. My damn sister."

"She didn't tell you anything?"

"No. She stayed close with Meema, but Meema never breathed a word, and I can't even call her ghost to ask her." Desdemona's voice broke a little. That was because Meema had been dragged to Hell—the actual Hell—and tossed into the River of Souls. There was no coming back from that.

"Well, see what Gran might know, since she doesn't consider you 'the damned Deadwoods' anymore."

We both laughed.

"All right. I'll let your mom know that you're safe. But that you haven't told me where, and that you're not going to."

"Hey, did Deirdre find the hedge witch?"

"You know about that?"

"I saw it on the boards."

"No, but that's not quite a dead end either. We can talk later, when things are calmer." Her tone indicated this was not up for discussion. "Love you," she said.

"Love you," I said.

We hung up.

"Your aunts sound nice," Tuesday said.

"They are. Completely nuts, fond of yelling, and awesome. Now, let's get a bed for you and drag it downstairs. It's going to be dawn before we know it."

We spent the rest of the night moving things, getting things sorted. My cappuccino maker took up an entire side of the limited counter space in the kitchen. I'd need to get it its own table, but it would bide for now. When the sun was nearly rising, Tuesday went down to the cellar, and I fell into the bed in the room upstairs. I slept the entire day, not waking until Tuesday was standing over me.

"Oh, god, coffee. And food. I haven't even thought of shopping."

"There's a grocery store here in town. And you had a package delivered already."

"I did?" It must be the sign.

"Yes," she said. "What first?"

"Food. And then the grocery store. And then we need to do some shopping."

"I don't know that we'll have much of a selection here."

"Online shopping," I said. "They bring it to us."

"Very well. I'm going to go out and see what the feeding situation looks like," she said.

"Okay," I said. I needed to get one more thing from Baby into the house. I'd left it in the car, not sure what to do with it. I'd gone through the notes Caleb had left me, and he mentioned that there was a false wall in the office area, big enough for a safe. At least, I hoped it was.

When Tuesday left, I hustled down to the garage, thanking my lucky stars we didn't have to do our moving out on the sidewalk. I got the safe I'd bought off the classified inside, and went looking for the false wall. After a couple of false starts, I found it. The safe fit, barely. I opened it, making sure my cash stash was still there, and the Volcanic.

The temptation to kill Delgado was strong. But if I did that, the entire supernatural world would be looking for me. And the very thing that Caleb feared most would happen—it would end up in the hands of someone who shouldn't have it.

I'd have to find another way to off the obnoxious prick.

Remembering what had happened back in my office, I pulled the safe out. Then I went digging through the desk in the office, a monster of metal and wood that weighed about a thousand pounds, and found some brown manila envelopes. I wrapped the Volcanic in three of them, and returned to the false wall. Inspecting the inside, it went back deeper into the wall than the safe. I thought this must be over the stairway that led to the cellar, and made up the wall of the garage. I crawled in, dug around a little, and made a hole for the Volcanic. Then I tucked it in, covered it with rock, and then some more rock, and then even more. I stopped only because I wanted to be able to snug the safe back in, and thought I might be getting a little overzealous.

The Volcanic had that effect on me, though.

The safe fit, and I locked it after taking out a decent sized wad of cash for the upcoming shopping. I fitted the wall slats of the chair rail back into place. Thank god for bead board. The seams were barely noticeable.

On inspection, I moved the monster desk, sweating my ass off in the process, in front of the false wall. It covered it up well.

When Tuesday came back, she was surprised to see me. "What have you been doing? You're a mess."

"Just some work here in the office."

"Now? What about food?"

"Let me go get the spiders out of my hair, and I'm off." I didn't want to field her questions. I didn't want to explain anything about Caleb, and I sure as hell wasn't going to tell her about the Volcanic. But the desk and false wall were right over her bed, so I'd need to open it when she was out.

That was something to make a note of. Maybe someday I could tell her, but not today.

CHAPTER TWENTY

I HEADED OUT FIFTEEN MINUTES LATER, STOPPING AT A tiny café to get the best green chili burrito I'd ever had, and then went to the grocery store. Even though I was full to waddling, I still bought more than I probably needed, given that I was the only one eating.

I didn't care. I hadn't thought about food as more than something I needed to do from time to time for the last two weeks, and given that I love to eat, that was a hardship.

When I got back, Tuesday helped me bring in the groceries. Just as we finished putting them away, my phone rang.

It was Mom. "Deana, you're on speaker."

"Okay, I'm doing the same. I want Tuesday to be up to speed as well."

"Is that the vampire who has been helping you?" Deirdre asked.

"Yes," Tuesday said.

"Thank you," Deirdre replied. "We appreciate it."

"Deana is a good person. I am glad to," Tuesday said.

"Thank you," I said to her.

She nodded.

"Enough with the love fest," Daniella said. "We've got the body on the way home. We're posting online about the injustice done to our family, so you can read it, but don't you dare respond in any way. It's a bit over the top," she finished. "Deirdre wrote it."

"It's perfect," Gran said. "We're throwing the most amazing wake Deadwood has ever seen."

"Someone will need to video it for me," I said.

"And we're buying a new cappuccino maker," Mom said.

Tuesday and I looked at each other and burst out laughing.

"I'm glad I didn't bet against you," she said. "You were right about your mom."

"What's so funny?" Mom sounded aggrieved. "I can't believe that thing didn't survive."

"It did," I said, trying to catch my breath. "I took it with me."

"You little shit," Mom said. "You took it, and were planning to leave us to come home to nothing?" Her voice rose.

Which made Tuesday and I laugh even harder.

"Dare I ask?" Daniella said.

"I'll explain later," Gran told her. "Dee, be glad it's still alive. Even if it has been stolen!" That last bit was for me.

"Well at least it didn't melt into a puddle of goo," I said. "I'm a damned hero."

"Now that we've solved the coffee concerns, can we get to the matter at hand?" Daniella asked. "You can't be Deana Holliday anymore. Not since you're supposed to be dead."

"Oh, shit," I said.

"Yeah, I wondered if you thought about that," Deirdre said. "But never fear. The aunties have sorted it for you. DeAnna has agreed to let it be known that she was a bit indiscreet in younger years, and gave a daughter up for adoption. You are her other grand-daughter, but you won't be discovered until sometime next year."

"You okay with that, Gran?" I asked.

"I am. Now I asked that she be named Deana, according to our family tradition, and she was. But when she had a daughter, she said that she'd be damned if she was going to name her kid after people she didn't know."

"So who am I?" I asked.

"Delilah Night," Desdemona said. "You'll be able to change your name once the family reunion occurs."

"That's a good idea," Tuesday chimed in. "Unless you'd already considered this?" She asked me.

"Nope, hadn't even thought about it. What happened to my rebel mom?"

"She died of cancer. Before she died, she told you about her adoption, and said that if you wanted to find your family, she wouldn't mind," Daniella chimed in.

"You all seem quite comfortable with this sort of thing," Tuesday remarked.

"We have to die and reinvent ourselves regularly," Desdemona said. "I'm my own great granddaughter."

"Clever," Tuesday said.

"Necessary," Deirdre replied. "Deana, I'll need to know where to send the papers for your new identity. I'll think about how Deana and her cousin met, too. Just to make everything easier to move over."

"Well, there goes our anonymity," Tuesday said.

"We're not going to tell anyone," Gran snapped.

"82 Main Street, in Bisbee, Arizona."

There was a silence, and then Mom said, "Good grief. What are you doing there?"

"It's a long story. But it's perfect," I said.

"I'll get them out tomorrow," Deirdre said. "Express, so you don't have to wait. Lay low until then, will you please?"

"I will," I promised.

We chatted a bit more, and then ended the call. Tuesday looked at me. "This is becoming more complicated."

"I didn't even think about how I was going to live if

everyone thought I was dead," I confessed. "I'm glad they did."

"I'll need to start thinking of you as Delilah so I don't slip."

"I'll need to the same."

The papers arrived the next day. Whoever their forger was, my aunts had a great connection. I was able to get a driver's license, although I wasn't sure what to do with all my vehicles. Shit. But it was another complication that could be worked out.

I was from Kokomo, Indiana, and I'd moved here for a change. This was going to take some time to get used to.

But I'd do it. Because there were things to do, and people to bring to justice. The cost of my name was a small price to pay.

It was another week before I was ready to go public as Delilah Knight. I found that I was nervous, and couldn't sit still. I'd started to transfer my life over from Deana to Delilah, but it was slow going.

Tuesday helped me at night, cleaning the place until it gleamed, and given its original shape, that was saying something. Finally, there was no more reason to delay. I pulled out the sign I'd ordered on a whim when we were in Yuma.

"You want to help me put this up?" I asked.

We hung it in the window, fiddling with the chains until it was level, and perfect. It took up most of the window, but I could still see out around the neon. "Let's turn it on," I said. I ducked back inside, and turned on the switch. The pink and white of the neon sign lit up the window.

Going back out to the sidewalk, I smiled when I saw it.

"What does it mean?" Tuesday asked.

I realized I hadn't explained the snide remark that Madigan had made when he blew up my office. I also realized that I hadn't told her that it was Madigan that blew up my office.

"Tuesday, why did you agree to come with me?"

"Because I felt it was good for both of us. You needed to get out of town, and upon reflection, so did I. You're never going to get rid of the vampires who are interested in you, even after you reappear as Delilah. You need someone who is part of that world, that you can trust, with you. How are you going to explain having Deana's car, and bikes?"

"I've been thinking about that, and I think I can take a page out of the aunts' book."

"More subterfuge."

"Hey, Miss living under the radar of society. You don't get to throw shade my way," I said, but without any heat. "Can I trust you?"

"Do you not think so?"

"I think so, but I'm scared."

She looked at me for a moment. "Shall I make an oath to you?"

"Is that wise?" I had no idea what it meant, I mean,

to vampires. It sounded serious.

"Give me your hand."

"Are you going to bite me? Right here, on the street?"

"Oh, all right. Come inside," she huffed.

We walked into the office, and she held out her hand. I gave her mine, and she bit it, a thin prick in the middle of my hand. Then she bit her own, and clasped our hands together. "I swear, on our shared blood, that I will not hurt you, or work against you. I am your friend, and your ally, Deana Holliday. Do you accept my oath?"

Wow. "Yes, I do."

"Then consider it done. If I should break it, all you need to do is find a vampire and tell them of this. I will pay for breaking my oath."

"You didn't have to do this," I said.

"No, I did. We are friends. I have made the choice to be here, to be your friend. And I hope that you are mine. You can trust me."

I sighed. "Then sit down." I told her almost everything—that Madigan wanted something I couldn't find for him, and when I told him it wasn't happening, he blew up my office, as well as the rest of the strip mall for good measure.

"And when he left, the smarmy shit, he told me he'd kept his word, that he hadn't closed me down. I was just mostly closed."

She stared at me, and started to laugh.

"What?" I asked.

"Being your friend is never going to be dull, is it?"

"Probably not, despite my best efforts."

After that, she went out to feed—there was a concert down the street at the little theater, and she was pretty sure she could zip around and get plenty with the crowd. I turned off the light, and went to bed.

The next morning, I got up and felt refreshed. While I hadn't unburdened myself totally—I couldn't, because of the pact I'd made with Caleb—I had a friend. An ally. When questioned, she hadn't hesitated.

I got a shower, and went down to my office, taking great pleasure in turning on the sign. In fact, I was so pleased, I had to go out on the sidewalk and look at it again. It looked just as good in the daytime as it had at night.

The Mostly Open Investigative Agency.

"Delilah Knight, Owner," I said out loud.

How long I stood there, I didn't know, but I was starting to get hot in the morning sun when I made myself go in. I took out my laptop and spent the morning closing out all my Deana accounts. I made a note to remind the aunts that they'd done this for their dearly departed niece.

Then I created all new accounts—although I had some already on social media sites, thanks to my aunts' diligence in making Delilah have a life—and registered my business on the Arizona state website. I took out an ad in the Bisbee paper.

And for nearly two days, I enjoyed the idea that I

was safe for the time being. That I had a family, and a friend, and a plan. I was in control of my life once more. If anyone tried to come and take it from me again, I'd have their ass.

Although maybe I'd need to do a little planning on the Madigan front. He was strong, and it would take some major effort to go up against him again. But I knew he'd find me eventually. The next time, however, I wouldn't be someone he'd throw against a wall. That was for damn sure.

The next morning, I got up with an inclination to bake. Today it was Shepherd's Pie. I'd never eaten it myself, but after the experience with Kel, I wasn't going to ignore the urge. I did wonder, however, who the Shepherd's Pie would bring in. If my suspicion was correct.

Just like before, I made the pie, cut it, and brought it down to the office, setting it with some plates and forks on the coffee bar. And I waited.

I'd put an old fashioned brass bell on the door, liking the sound of it when I found it in antique shop down the street. The bell jingled, and a young girl with a wild, nearly feral look came in.

"Are you Delilah Knight?" she asked. "And wow, it smells delicious in here."

"I am," I said as I got up with a smile. "Welcome to the Mostly Open. How can I help you?"

THE EVENTS that Deana refers to as having happened in Deadwood are from another book, Hellborn, which is Book One of The Deadwood Sisters: The Unlucky. You can find that here, and meet her Deadwood aunties, as well as more of her mom and gran.

Book Two of The Deadwood Sisters: The Unlucky is Hellfire, and it's coming out in September of 2019. In October, Dark Night, Book Two of the Mostly Open Paranormal Investigative Agency will be out. Click on the links and they'll take you right to them. (Keep reading for a sneak peak of the first chapter of Hellborn.)

These two series—The Deadwood Sisters, and the Mostly Open Paranormal Investigative Agency—are about a great family, the Nightingales who are also Hollidays. They have a lot of family baggage, as you might have figured out from Deana's running commentary about Deadwood. Which they are totally okay with. Except for the secrets. And the lies. And the demons. And the curse. But hey—they're working on it!

You can also click onto my Author Page to see all the books and sign up for my Newsletter to keep up with all the things coming.

I love these women. I hope you do too.

XOXO,
Lisa

SMOKIN' HAWT CHERRY CHIPOTLE PIE

Ingredients

Pie

1 1/2 cups confectioners' sugar
1/4 cup flour
1/2 teaspoon ground cinnamon
1 chipotle pepper, canned
1 teaspoon balsamic vinegar
1/4 teaspoon almond extract
3 pounds frozen pitted dark sweet cherries
1 Honey Maid graham cracker crust pie shell

Crumble topping

½ Cup all-purpose flour
¼ cup brown sugar packed
¼ cup butter
Directions:

Thaw and drain cherries.

Remove the seeds from the chipotle pepper and chop to a fine consistency.

Heat the oven to 400°F.

Mix the confectioners' sugar, flour, and cinnamon in a large mixing bowl. Stir in the chipotle pepper, vinegar, almond extract, and cherries until all of the dry ingredients have been moistened.

Fill the pre-made crust with the cherry mixture.

Mix crumble ingredients together with a fork until crumbly. Top the pie filling with crumble mixture.

Bake for approximately 50 minutes until the crumble is golden brown.

Cool 15-20 minutes.

Adapted to Deana's tastes from the Homemade in a Hurry Cookbook

SNEAK PEAK OF HELLBORN

THE SOUND OF BREAKING CHINA ECHOED AROUND THE house as I slammed out the front door. I made sure to slam the screen door hard, just to make a point.

"Damn woman," I muttered.

"I heard that!"

"Good!" I yelled over my shoulder. "I wanted you to!" I stomped to my car, pulling my keys from my pocket. As I got into the car, I pulled my hair up into a messy bun. I caught sight of myself in the mirror. Dark brown hair, brownish green eyes, and the nose ring. I couldn't get used to it, but I needed it to look like someone else. The only thing that would cure me now was to race down the road in my Porsche 911. Speed was a universal healer.

Or killer, if you weren't careful. But it didn't matter. I couldn't die. More's the damn pity. The nose ring sparkled in the sunlight. Having to look like someone else was one of the joys of not being able to die. "I hate my life!" I made sure to yell out the window.

"I heard that!" came from the house again.

As I gunned the engine, I saw our neighbor, Mrs. Kittrick, glaring. She hated us. And for this, she'd probably call the cops. Noise complaints were her favorite bitch move. Like we didn't have Sturgis here every damn year. But gotta call the po-po on those Nightingale ... women.

That's how she referred to us. Those Nightingale... women. You could feel the pause. I knew that she wanted to call us whores. But she couldn't bring herself to do it. As the supposed daughter of myself, I was another one in a long line of those ... women.

Which made me nice as pie to her. It nearly killed the old bat.

"Hi, Mrs. Kittrick!" I called out the window as I pulled away from the house. "Your yard is gorgeous, as usual!" I waved like we weren't bitter foes and grinned as I looked in the rear-view mirror to see her glaring at my amazing gunmetal gray automotive ass.

That simple act of petty kindness alone eased my anger and brought it down to a non-killing level.

My sisters were enough to make anyone homicidal on a normal day. Add my mom to the mix, and it was a miracle that our house was still standing. Four women who were never, ever wrong was challenging on a good day. The small fact that we'd been here for over one hundred and twenty years didn't help, either.

That whole 'can't die' thing was a pain in my ass. But if we left the area, we lost the immortal factor that had allowed us to live here and threaten one another for over a century. We'd only had one of my sisters leave the Deadwood area, and she'd died over sixty years ago. The rest of us stayed here, fussing and fighting, as my mom said.

As I left the neighborhood, and got out onto the highway, I hit the gas, letting the RPMs vent all my frustration. Normally, my family and I resolved our disagreements easily, being skilled practitioners at the sport, but not this time. This one was too big.

You can't just ignore it when a necromancer moves into your street. You just can't. They have their craft, like everyone else. But their craft involves the dead. That's where they get their power from—the dead. Hence the 'necro' part of necromancer.

Not to mention I'd never met a single necromancer who did his thing for the good of humanity. Nope. They were always self-centered. Usually raging narcissists, and they exploited the dead. Generally, the dead want to be left in peace, but necromancers are based in holding up that process.

So ... no. No ignoring the friendly neighborhood necromancer. Not on my watch.

My mom—known as Meema--didn't agree. She'd been the one throwing the china at me as I left. My sisters, Deirdre and Daniella, didn't feel strongly one way or the other, which was miraculous, but they were tired. We'd had a busy month with a warlock and the tea shop. So they took the path of least resistance.

Which wasn't the path I was advocating. It had escalated from there. Meema wanted to wait and see if he managed to make things troublesome.

I hated to wait and see. This meant that any pets in the neighborhood would disappear suddenly, at the very least. The dead liked to eat when brought back by necromancers. Cats were a favorite. So were nosy dogs.

Not that we had any. But our neighbors did. I didn't even want Mrs. Kittrick's two evil old cats to get eaten. We had a house chicken, but I'd back Evil against a zombie any day of the week.

Three against one meant we were going to wait and see. I didn't understand why we couldn't just go introduce ourselves, and let him know the rules, mainly: One Strike And You're Out.

I shook my head as I blasted down the highway, Bowie wailing from the speakers. This was just making more work for us. We'd have to start a regular patrol of the cemeteries immediately. That was a shit ton of extra work. Keeping the supernatural side of Deadwood, South Dakota on the rails was enough.

As I got closer to the Wyoming border, I realized that this wasn't going to solve my problem. I made a giant loop of a U-turn at the next exit ramp and headed back to Deadwood. But I wasn't going to head home. I'd stop at the Saloon No. 10 and get a Crab Hollandaise burger and a whiskey. Maybe a couple of whiskeys.

Comfort food before heading back to face my dragon family.

Not real dragons, or anything like that. Although there were dragons still around. I'd heard of some hiding out down in the Southwest. No dragons in my family. We had enough problems with being witches. Immortality, as long as we never left Deadwood. We could all see ghosts.

And we all had a finely tuned sense of right and wrong. All of us did things to even the playing field, make things square. Meema called it our justice-meter. We also looked out for Deadwood. Granny, long gone, had laid down the law. We protected Deadwood from all the supernatural shit that liked to try and park here and do whatever it was that was on their agenda. It was never anything good for the humans that lived here. Granny had felt coming to Deadwood had not only changed her life but saved it. Looking out for Deadwood was the family business.

Oh, and we had a ghost. A family ghost. Who might even rate higher on the pain-in-the ass scale than my mother and sisters right now.

John Henry Holliday. My grandfather. Yeah, *that* John Henry Holliday.

It was a shame he was already dead. On days like today, I wanted to kill him. This was all John's fault. He and my mother had gotten into it about something— neither would tell us what, which made it worse—and Meema was on a rampage. Another thing that would need to be sorted. There were too many secrets in our house. I shook my head. Later. This would all need to happen later.

Deadwood was quiet today. It was late spring. We had a little more time before the tourists descended en masse on us. Not that I was complaining. I loved the tourists. I didn't know them, and despite the public family business, didn't get to know them. But I loved them nonetheless.

Because it was late spring, Meema closed Monday through Wednesday. I could roll right past our family's tea and herbal shop without feeling any guilt. Thank goddess, because the Crab Hollandaise burger was calling to me in the worst way. I parked and walked in, taking a seat at the bar.

Duffy, the bartender, looked over her shoulder when I sat down. "Hey, Des, what's up?"

I rolled my eyes. "Fighting with Meema and my sisters. What else?"

"Crab?"

"Yes, please." I loved being a local.

Outside of the fact that all I had to do was walk in here, and the bartenders knew what I was having, I loved Deadwood. I wouldn't want to be anywhere else. The fact that who and what I was centered on Deadwood came in second, almost. I truly loved it here.

"What are you drinking?"

"The Stranahan," I said. I loved that they had a good-sized whiskey selection. Even though I didn't stray from my favorites. Right now, it was the Colorado whiskey from the Stranahan down in Denver.

Duffy smiled and poured me a healthy shot, neat. She added a glass of water, and then let me be.

Yeah, it was good to be local.

I stared at the mirrors over the bar, not really seeing them. Someone came in the door, and I felt the breeze from the open door waft over me. Kind of like when you felt ghosts pass by. That was another reason I liked Saloon No. 10. I knew the ghosts here, and they knew me. Actually, a number of them had known me. As the oldest granddaughter of Desdemona Nightingale, saloon and dance hall girl at the Bella Union Saloon, circa 1876, she and my mom, also Desdemona Nightingale, had seen a lot of death. So had I, Desdemona Nightingale number three.

But since we all knew each other, the ghosts here tended to leave me alone unless they were in the mood for a chat. They were terrible gossips. After a hundred years, I was pretty good about ignoring ghosts I didn't want to deal with.

Duffy came out with a plate and set it in front of me. "Here you go, sweets."

"Thanks, Duff." I smiled.

I inhaled the smell of crab and hollandaise. Two of the foods from the goddess. I took a bite and as I was chewing, steps sounded behind me. The proverbial boots-on-hardwood.

"Desdemona Holliday," a deep voice said.

I chewed carefully and swallowed. Then I set my burger down, also carefully. I wiped my hands on my napkin and took a deep breath. I felt the magic gather at my fingers. No one called us Holliday. We were the Nightingales, and the Holliday aspect was kept under wraps.

No exceptions.

I turned my barstool around slowly to see what had to be the brand-new neighbor, since the man in front of me was a necromancer. While he didn't have the normal stink they all seemed to have, he had the look. After a while, you could just tell. He was tall, with dark, longish hair. His face was clean-shaven, and his eyes were the gray-green of a summer storm.

What the hell? Stop it, I told myself. This guy needed to shape up, move, or die. No matter what color his eyes were.

We protected Deadwood. No exceptions.

"I am Desdemona Nightingale. Can I help you?" The magic coiled tightly in my fingers, waiting to be released. One wrong move, pal. Make just one ... and all my aggression is gone for the day. Probably for tomorrow, too.

He frowned. "You call yourselves Nightingale, but we both know the truth."

"Oh? Well, please enlighten me." I swiveled a half-turn and picked up my burger again. "I suppose you can have a seat." I indicated the stool next to me with my burger.

"I did not come here to—"

"I came here for this burger, and I'm not letting it get cold. Sit, or don't." I turned the barstool back to the bar. It was a risk, putting my back to him, but it was better he not suspect anything. Bad enough he knew my real name.

The indecision rolled off him. That was a good sign. At least he didn't plan to off me before I finished the burger. Then he sat down.

"What can I do for you?" I asked.

"I wish to make peace with you."

"I don't understand what you're talking about." The magic waiting in my hands eased in intensity. I didn't know what he wanted, but it seemed there wasn't going to be a showdown at the Saloon No. 10. Which was probably for the best. Damn it.

"I am well aware of what you and your family do here."

My eyebrow went up. I knew it made me seem snotty as hell, but I couldn't help it. "Are you? Then why are you here?"

"My help has been requested."

Oh, this was good. "In what way?" Finishing the burger, I went to work on the fries.

"I would like the chance to help those requesting my ... services without interference from you."

"Really? I'd like all the cats and dogs in our neighborhood to keep on breathing."

"That's not—"

"It's totally realistic and fair, zombie guy," I hissed, leaning closer to him. "And you know it. If you know about my family, then you know better than to come here and try and blow smoke at me."

"We're not all the same."

I laughed. "Yeah, sure. I've met a bunch of you, and yes, you are all the same. It's part of the job description."

He flushed, the color spreading up from his neck into his cheeks. "That's a matter of choice."

"Which totally sells your profession even more, zombie guy."

"I have a name," he grumbled.

"Do I need it?"

"Seeing as we're neighbors, it would be neighborly if you knew it."

"Lay it on me."

"Zane McCallister."

I nodded. "And how long do you plan to stay, Zane McCallister?"

"Depends," he said.

"What can I get you?" Duffy chose this moment to come over, making eyes at me.

Smiling, I gave a little shake with my head. She'd bounce him if I wanted, but I could handle this.

"An iced tea, please." Zane smiled pleasantly at Duffy.

Duffy nodded and moved away.

"Depends on what?" I asked.

"On exactly what my client needs. After that?" He shrugged, making no promises.

"Who is your client? I know most of the dead guys around here."

He gave me a glance that I couldn't interpret. "Yes, I think you probably know this one well."

"Oh?"

"John Holliday."

Damn that man straight to hell.

Get your copy of Hellborn HERE.

ABOUT THE AUTHOR

USA TODAY BESTSELLING AUTHOR

LISA MANIFOLD

FANTASY ACTION
MYSTERY LOVE

Lisa Manifold is a *USA Today* Bestselling Author of fantasy, paranormal, and romance stories. She moved to Colorado as an adult and has no plans of living anywhere else. She is a consummate reader, often running late because "Just one more page!" She is a fan of all things Con, and has an entire room devoted to the costumes created for Cons.

Lisa is the author of many flavors of paranormal series, including The Realm, Djinn Everlasting, Dragon Thief, The Aumahnee Prophecy, Tales from the Veil, Sisters of the Curse, the books from The Midnight Coven collective, and the upcoming Deadwood Sisters and The Mostly Open Paranormal Investigative Agency.

She lives as close to the mountains as possible with her husband, children, and four red rescue dogs.

Stay in touch:
Sign up for my Newsletter and never miss a thing!
Website: www.lisamanifold.com
Or one of the links below.

ALSO BY LISA MANIFOLD

Vampire Mates

(with The Midnight Coven)

Immortal Darkness (Aug 2019)

The Mostly Open Paranormal Investigative Agency

Dark Pact

Dark Night (Oct 2019)

Vampire Brides

(with The Midnight Coven)

Forever Blood

Deadwood Sisters

Hellborn: The Unlucky Book 1

Hellfire: The Unlucky Book 2 (Sept 2019)

Dragon Thief

Dragon Lost

Dragon Found

The Realm Series

Heart of the Goblin King

To Wed the Goblin King

Realms of the Goblin King

Rise of the Dragon King

The Companion Tales, Volume I

The Companion Tales, Volume II

The Aumahnee Prophecy

with Corinne O'Flynn

Eamonn's Tale

Marigold's Tale

Watchers of the Veil

Defenders of the Realm

Tales From The Veil

with Corinne O'Flynn

The Portal Keepers

The Gimcrackers

Djinn Everlasting

Three Wishes

Forgotten Wishes

Hidden Wishes

Sisters of the Curse

Thea's Tale

One Night at the Ball

Casimir's Journey

Do you like being in the loop? Sign up for Lisa's newsletter! Shenanigans, book recs, and the latest news abound!

www.ingramcontent.com/pod-product-compliance
Lightning Source LLC
Chambersburg PA
CBHW031026260626
47153CB00017B/2254